CW00717730

EDITH CORY-KING   **ABOUT THE AUTHOR**

After an unforgettable week digging up stone handaxes at a site in Kenya, the author retained an interest in prehistory for the rest of her life.

Having spent twenty-five years in Tanzania, she combined the interest and her knowledge of East Africa to write 'My Ancestors walked out of Africa'.

Other books the author has written are 'Trunkful of Letters' (with G. Hine), 'Belgravia or Mwanza' (with V. Ngalinda), 'Tanzan Tales' and 'Asante Mamsapu'.

Copyright © 2010 Edith Cory-King

First Published in Paperback in 2010

Apart from any use permitted under UK Copyright law, this publication may only be reproduced, stored, or transmitted, in any form, or by any means, with prior permission in writing of the publishers or, in the case of reprographic production, in accordance with the terms of licenses issued by the Copyright Licensing Agency.

All characters and scenarios in this publication are fictitious and any resemblance to real persons, living or dead, is purely coincidental.

ISBN: 978-1-84944-037-0

British Library Cataloguing in Publication Data.
A catalogue record for this book is available from the British Library.

Published by UKUnpublished.

UKUnpublished
.CO.UK

www.ukunpublished.co.uk
info@ukunpublished.co.uk

MY ANCESTORS WALKED OUT OF AFRICA

By

EDITH CORY-KING

SERPENT

Baratu looked around him at the brown, barren, hot landscape strewn with small stones and rocks. Thorn bushes grew dotted about and the larger acacia species degenerated into stunted trees. This was the area where fossils could be found, therefore he walked with a light tread, glancing closely at everything in his path and beyond.

Sometimes he had a sensation as if they spoke to him, the fossils, ancient hominins, with faraway voices sounding like whispering so that he never heard individual words. It was then he was most likely to make a find and as the leader of the African fossil team, this resulted in his scoring the greatest number of discoveries. It was as if the distant voices wanted him to find something that had once belonged to them, their fossilised bones. But what was strange about that? After all, these hominins were his ancestors. Had not numerous scientists proved that the earliest humans developed in Africa, and as an African himself, he was surely the one in line for contact if that was what they wanted. Of course it was something he could not discuss with the others, not even his boss, 'the Lady Archaeologist' as she was known. That word 'palaeoanthropologist' was much too long for most tongues.

He walked concentrating his mind on the task in hand, his eyes half-closed against the glare of the sun, observing tiny shadows that might betray a fossil washed out of the soil. That was the way his companions in the camp went fossil hunting but he – there it was again. Baratu turned to look back in case those fellow prospectors were in sight and he was merely hearing their chatter. No, the terrain was empty. Faintly, ever so faintly, the voices talked, a sound as if borne by a wind when none was blowing. He stopped in his tracks, and rooted to the spot, turned all the way round looking closely at the ground by his feet. Then he widened the circle until on the last sweep he saw it.

A closer look revealed the end of what might turn out to be a jawbone. The colour and shape were right for a fossil, possibly hominin. He piled a few bigger stones near it, drew out his compass and took a bearing back to camp noting the opposite direction.

That evening at the agreed schedule the boss came up on the radiophone. 'Anything to report?'

'You had better come, I think I have found something important.'

The Lady Archaeologist arrived on the small supply plane next day, grey haired, sunburnt, with a soft sunhat shading her eyes. Baratu and the fossil team accompanied her to the find. She knelt on the hard-baked soil by the pile of stones and bent over the small object protruding from the ground. Chipping away tiny particles of earth with a dental tool she dug as gently as the real practitioner.

'A jawbone!' she exclaimed triumphantly.

The team looked at one another each with the same question in mind. Was the rest of the fossil skull somewhere near, the whole skeleton or at least some remaining fossil bones? They bent over the spot, watching with suspense to see the find gradually brought to light in the twenty-first century.

— — — — — —

There was no one else to play with and in his boredom the heap of granite boulders beckoned an adventure. Smooth, curved like giant eggs, they made climbing difficult. He slithered off again and again until he managed to scramble onto the protruding dome of one buried in the ground. From that slightly elevated position he peered over the top of its neighbour and came face to face with a leopard. Stretched out on a rock ledge shaded by a gnarled tree the animal looked at him with interest, and so close was he that Toma squinted to meet its gaze.

Trying to beat a hasty retreat his podgy hands lost their grip, he fell off his perch, tumbled to a stop against the twigs of an acacia bush, and curled up with his head tucked in waiting for the animal to pounce and dig its claws into his back. Instead it was thorns that pierced his skin but he did not dare call out. Vaguely he remembered his bigger brother being attacked by an animal jumping from behind bushes. It had carried him away swiftly. Toma had heard his screams diminishing with distance while he sat frozen with fright.

Now he continued to keep still even when he heard his mother calling and did not stir until he found himself in his father's arms. He clung to the big male's neck and wound his legs as best he could around the hairy body.

Back at the camp his father set him on his feet. 'Buhu?' he asked.

Toma still terror-stricken whimpered, 'Boo-boo,' unable yet to pronounce the word for animal properly. The big male, growling angrily, picked up his throwing sticks but on reaching the rocks the predator was gone.

Toma held his arms out to his mother for a cuddle. The female, heavily pregnant and therefore unwilling to lift him up, pushed the child away gently and diverted his attention by handing him a twig he could carry in imitation of her short digging stick. Picking up her pouch as well, she led him from the camp to gather food.

They walked away busying themselves with turning stones and capturing beetles and their larvae, as well as larger spiders sheltering from the heat despite the late afternoon. They did not pick up centipedes or millipedes always sour to taste. Toma went off on his own short excursions after rats, too fast to let him catch them by the tail, but he managed to find a nest of ratlings that his mother scooped into the stiff leather food pouch.

There were few leaves on the bushes in this dry season and the fibrous tubers from which juice could be squeezed to quench their thirst were difficult to find. Dragging her feet the female moved ponderously, drowsily, in the still, shimmering heat, further and further from the campsite. A heavy tummy was nothing strange. Out of it had come a child. No not Toma but the one who had been killed. Then when her tummy grew large again it was Toma. This time there would be another. Regretfully she thought of the way her male insisted on moving camp every morning although she could hardly walk with its weight.

She removed the eggs from a nest fallen out of a bush and called to Toma to stay by her, then sat down exhausted. Where was Toma? Behind her busy catching insects. She beckoned for him to return to her side. Buhu could be very dangerous especially if they had a young one with them and she looked furtively about her, noticing how far they had come. Her thoughts returned to the child before Toma, bigger than him when the animal took him away. Toma was like Badili, always chasing something.

She heaved herself up and continued searching for things to eat they could take back to Joha. Bending down with difficulty she turned another stone and found a scorpion. No, they did not taste nice; she flicked it away with her stick. Loosening the baked soil round plants was hard work, and pulling them up for their edible roots sapped her strength but she must go on, there was not enough in her food pouch to feed the three of them. And it was so hot. Ahead stood a hillock of giant rocks promising cooler air in their shade. Toma had scampered off again running about in the near distance, seemingly catching something.

He was attempting to bag a lizard that scurried from one bush to another trying to find a hole. It was just a game, the lizard was too clever in its avoiding tactics to be caught. Then in front of him something moved, a snout protruded from a hole in the ground and Toma froze the way his father had taught him, standing still like a stump of a tree. The snout emerged further and further while Toma prepared to run if this buhu turned out to be a snake. His father had taught him never to play with that sort of flesh. After the very long snout emerged the head with longish ears, and then came a long body, short legs and a long thick tail. Toma, full of curiosity watched, and when he took a step towards the animal and it lumbered away, he hurried alongside to see it properly.

Meanwhile the female had reached the rocks and was clambering up slowly on a low one to take a rest in the shade of a fissure between stones looming above her. Something twisted itself round her ankles so that she fell onto her side still clutching the digging stick and pouch. Her legs were quickly bound together by slithering bonds and when she began to scream, most of her body had already disappeared within the black and grey coils of the python.

The boy hearing the screams stopped in his tracks. He looked up and saw the head of his mother protruding from something wound all round her. Her screams turned into intermittent shrieks as the coils began their work, constricting and pushing the breath out of her. Toma started to run towards the rocks and his mother but then stopped short and looked open-mouthed as her shrieks changed to choking sounds. Her head disappeared altogether inside the coils. There was a cracking of bones, then the whole thing lurched into the cleft.

The boy's mouth quivered, he let out a howl and turning on his heels fled from the place. He ran and ran, his legs strong already and well used to long walks carried him some distance before he slowed to a walk. He could not understand what had happened and only knew he must get back to Joha.

The savannah glowed with heat, small animals had retreated into their holes and big ones rested in whatever shade they could find. Toma met none of them and unhindered walked, ran and jogged in imitation of his father. He grew thirsty and hungry but was too intent on flight to pick up what was edible around him. The sun moved further down the sky, its rays less fierce, the ground still radiating heat.

Parched, hunger-driven and still terrified he ran on until he came to a tree. By now the sun was setting, orange then lilac clouds tinted the landscape as daylight changed swiftly into night. For Toma the tree was like the one at camp he had already attempted to climb and he managed to pull himself up between two branches forming a fork. A feeling of relative safety came over him and when he became drowsy, he turned on his tummy. As tiredness grew, his limbs dangled loose but the broad branch supported the body preventing it from sliding off. Shock, exhaustion and the dark found him a deep sleep.

Joha had made camp early that day to help the female who could hardly keep up with him any longer. They had seen no buhu on their way, the vegetation was dry and unpalatable and the riverbed almost empty except for muddy puddles soiled by animals. It was necessary for her to go foraging again and he too had left after her departure, following the direction of vultures he could see flying over what might be a kill. It turned out to be a dying newly born antelope probably abandoned by the mother. He hit it on the head with his cudgel, cut through its skin with his stone handaxe for a few morsels to satisfy his hunger, and shouldered it back to camp to hang on the tree by a longish thong, off the ground so that hyenas could not reach it and out of the way of tree climbing leopards.

When the sun sank lower and his mate and child still had not returned, he became anxious for their safety and set out to find them, breaking into a jog and reading the ground for the direction they had taken. Being used to tracking he followed their trail by the signs they had left, a hole where his mate had dug, a broken stem, scars on bushes where she had stripped off leaves, stones turned showing darker earth where they had lain.

He found the rocky hillock and lost the trail. Here they must have climbed up; here something happened but without any sign of blood. The fissure which looked like an animal's lair was empty. There was no flesh, hair, nail, or tooth anywhere, impaled on a thorn or lying on the ground - no sign of struggle. Nothing he could read. Retracing his way along the track made by his mate going towards the rocks, the child's more difficult to read because it meandered back and forth, he finally found clear signs of small running feet going off in one direction: Toma's.

He grunted with satisfaction but then stopped, frowned, looked closely at the toe and heel marks in the loose soil realising something was badly wrong. The female could not have allowed the child to run off on his own. Had she been carried off by marauding males? He looked around aware suddenly that he might be in danger.

By this time the selfsame savannah sun which had lit up the terrain in subdued colours for Toma sank rapidly beneath the horizon allowing a short cooling twilight but then night descended, wiping out the further trail of his child. He sat down dispirited. Now there was no chance at all of finding his family. Anger welled up at the thought that he was now forced to hunt alone when a number of males fanning out earlier might have made the difference.

Seated on the ground making no movement, his ears were strained to catch the sound of feet or paws, of breathing or any noise made by a night predator. Starlight lit up the surroundings sufficiently for every bush to look like an approaching animal. A rustling near him made him tense his muscles for flight but then there was a squawk, just a night bird. He must look for its nest and eggs in the returning light of dawn. For now he had to sit waiting for that moment, waiting to find his child.

What chance was there of finding it alive? He felt heavy with foreboding. A buhu would surely get the scent of him, and then... His ears could almost hear the crunch of the little bones being broken by sharp teeth.

He shook his head to clear the sound, and stiff with fear for Toma, found the darker shadows looked increasingly menacing. When nothing moved he dozed only to wake with a start. He must not sleep with so many buhu probably prowling all around him. If only he could have stayed with his old family he would not be alone now. Why did the old males chase him away after a hunt when he had killed a buhu with twisted horns, and all by himself too? They were carrying the meat back to camp when the hunters stopped, pointed their throwing sticks at him and told him to go away. Even now in the dark he saw the scene vividly and felt his astonishment again. He thought they were pointing to something behind him until they started shouting, 'Go! Go!'

They were very menacing. Each time he asked why he should go they took up the throwing stance with their sticks raised. Then they walked off leaving him totally bewildered, only knowing they would kill him if he tried returning home.

But he did return. He still felt the defiance. Lonely and desperate he hid in tall reeds to peer between the stems watching to see what activity was going on in his old camp. Suddenly the stems were parted and a young female came creeping through the foliage. Afraid of discovery he leaped on her, stopped her shriek and carried her off as far as possible. When it felt safe he set her down, calmed her, offered food from his pouch and watched over her for several days in case she attempted to run back.

The thought of her and his subsequent mating brought him back to his loss. She had surely been carried off again, and Toma? Despite the dark, he could see the little face looming up and for a split second almost put his arms out to catch him. Then realising his mistake Joha felt even more dispirited though he could not bring himself to believe his son was dead - first Badili, now Toma.

Something rustled near him, his ears strained to pick up its direction. One of the shadows had moved - or had it? - making him grasp the throwing stick firmly in one hand and the cudgel in the other but the thing stayed put. He peered at it silhouetted against the sky to see if the buhu was merely keeping still in stalking him. It did not move and he shifted to face it squarely for a possible attack. Straining ears and eyes he grew tired and once more dozed off.

The cold wind sweeping across the savannah before dawn chilled Joha into waking. The buhu-bushes resumed their shape of branches and leaves, the sun returned, a huge orange ball already warming the land. He jumped up, grasped his hunting stick, ate the eggs from the night bird's nest and looked for Toma's trail.

The blades of grass his small feet might have trodden down had had time to straighten during the night, only pebbles repeatedly kicked aside, or a broken twig, or the imprint of toes or a heel still provided a clue. It was painstaking work and every time the trail was lost he retraced his steps to the last sign of disturbance and started again. What would he find? Not much, he thought.

He feared the sight of a mauled dismembered body and searched the sky for vultures. No sign of them probably meant Toma had already been completely eaten.

Joha stumbled on dejected, still reading the trail. In the distance a tree, one of the few in the landscape had something hanging from a fork, probably dead flesh put there by a leopard and he braced himself for the worst. He approached cautiously fearing the animal might still be in the grass below. As he had thought the thing in the tree was Toma and he looked dead. His father put a gentle hand on him and drew it back in shock. The body was warm, the child asleep. Even more gently he put an arm round him so that on waking he would not be frightened and lifted him off. Toma stirred, opened his eyes and flung his arms round his father, clinging to him as he struggled to awake.

A feeling, enormously powerful, overcame Joha so that he sat down and cradled his son in his arms holding him tight while tears rolled down his cheeks, and Toma seeing his father crying began to cry too.

BEING HUNTED

After the jawbone had been cleaned and catalogued it was ready for transportation to the Museum on the Lady Archaeologist's plane. She had persuaded Baratu that it was time he returned with her to visit his wife and children and so they flew, the precious box on her lap, across the African plateau back to the capital.

Baratu's wife and three children were overjoyed to see him. She cooked his favourite meal and the children clung to his hand and wanted to show him all their new clothes, schoolbooks and to tell him of their activities.

He had married a young woman and seeing her again he was aroused as men should be and that night had a long session of sex with her. She had at last consented to taking birth control pills: after all, three children were all he could afford if he was to carry out his plans for their secondary and university education.

Next day at the Museum's laboratory he found the Lady Archaeologist comparing the newly discovered jawbone with others in books. She told him it had belonged to a Homo erectus male and showed him some illustrations of how the hominin might have looked, rather hairy but nevertheless reasonably modern. Baratu had seen plenty of people walking the streets of the capital who could have passed for one. Old people especially, he thought, often reverted to looking somewhat prehistoric. In the picture the male represented by a head moulded by means of computer graphics was brown-eyed and brown-skinned.

My ancestor, thought Baratu, maybe his people are the ones I can hear. One thing he was certain of: he would never hear the voices of the robust type of prehistoric hominin who had big heads and teeth and probably could only make sounds not to be mistaken for words. Pictures drawn from fossil evidence showed them to have walked in a lumbering manner upright and yet still apelike. Once Homo erectus came on the scene the others seemed to have died out. Why? How could anyone know?

– – – – – –

Joha carried his child back to camp at a trot, joy still welling up in him that Toma was alive. There the realisation struck that his own food bag was almost empty and he no longer had his female to keep it stocked. A glance at the tree showed the flesh he had so carefully hung out of reach was gone, stolen by a buhu taking advantage of his night's absence.

Toma was already running up to the smooth rocks to attempt another climb despite his previous fright. The camp felt as empty to Joha as those many others he had occupied after being chased away by the fierce males and until the day he had captured the female. He looked about him to see if there was anything lying about of hers. Nothing! She had disappeared from his life but he had his child and he must feed it.

'Go,' said the voice in his ear. 'Go.'

There it was, that command he heard almost every dawn now, knowing there was nobody standing near who could have voiced it.

'Toma!' he called to the boy and when he came running swung him up to ride astride on his shoulders with his little arms and hands clasped round his father's forehead.

Joha squatted without upsetting the child's balance to picked up his hunting weapons and food pouch and strode from the camp following the voice's indicated direction. When a small buhu ran across, his handicap became apparent. Toma, set down on his sturdy feet, ran hither and thither exploring his surroundings and trying to catch edibles. Joha could not leave him for the time needed to stalk and kill an animal. They would have to live on foraging, relying on catching a slow-moving creature like a tortoise.

Watching his child scampering about at their resting places in any shade he could find, Joha thought of his female. She had been adept at finding tubers, fruits and nuts. He always looked forward to the food she handed him from her gathering pouch and when he remembered once again how willingly she had let him mate, he felt her loss even more keenly.

'The female good-good,' he told Toma who immediately put up his arms for a cuddle as he used to do with his mother. Joha enveloped him in a powerful hug murmuring, 'good-good' to soothe him.

He longed to have more children. 'Me want female,' he grunted determined to make a new effort to find one who might produce another Badili. He looked at Toma who, curled up in his arms, had gone to sleep and gently stroked back his hair that always fell over the child's forehead in an unruly tangle.

Placing Toma on the ground, he decided to renew his stone scraper while the boy slept. So far he had been unsuccessful at making anything like the sharp stone tool the big males had given him. He picked up some small rocks lying nearby and began chipping by striking one with another. The granite did not flake easily. The more Joha hammered it, the more only small chips came away. Toma awoke and put them between his toes and tried walking. Disgruntled at his own failure Joha gave up and turned his attention to finding a slim branch for another hunting stick, but the nearby tree was an acacia, twisted and gnarled, not a bough of any use.

'Bad-bad!' he exclaimed now thoroughly irritated, picked up his old stick, placed the cudgel in the skin pouch with handle sticking out, beckoned to Toma to pull the chips from his toes, and continued on the journey not knowing where he was going but somehow sure of the direction.

As Toma's legs grew longer and stronger he ran alongside Joha's big stride and picked up everything that looked edible, vomiting if his stomach rejected it. The drought had withered succulent leaves and tough ones growing low on branches were indigestible for him. Joha picked those higher up, chewed them and handed the wad to his child to eat.

The days were parching hot, the sun, a flaring white disk, reduced the azure of the sky to an insipid blue where clouds had fled elsewhere. Hippos and crocodiles no longer inhabited the river in which the only water was seepage collecting in pools. In the distance there were herds of elephants among islands of trees, or buffalo and antelopes grazing on patches of yellow dry grass above which circled ever-present vultures.

Many nights and days later, they rested in the shade of an acacia, eating pieces of very smelly hare meat from the skin pouch. Joha stepped away a little distance to relieve himself. As he squatted to defecate his eyes were drawn to another pair staring at him between stems of dry grass. Looking fixedly at the spot, the muzzle, ears and then a head became discernable in the pattern of the tree's shadow on the undergrowth. The eyes did not move, the stare was fixed, though for sure the buhu's body must be there, muscles tensed to leap.

Joha remained squatting for a moment not sure what to do. His child would be eaten after he had been killed and with that thought he rose very slowly to move backwards step by small step, never taking his eyes off the animal. Toma sensing danger and recognising his father's gait was unnatural, climbed onto a low branch and sat quite still. As Joha moved back, so the buhu emerged crouched and stalking, a long spotted body, a leopard. It crept forward keeping the distance between them.

With the hunting stick on the ground beyond his reach, Joha was defenceless and when his back bumped against the trunk of the tree, he waited body-taut for the inevitable attack. The leopard emerged fully from the undergrowth, an old beast, huge when seen so close up. Their mutual stare remained locked. Joha, aware of Toma above him, thought of the leopard pulling the child down to kill it and was seized with fury at his own helplessness. Standing absolutely still he prepared to use his hands and glared into the yellow eyes in a head he knew to be full of sharp teeth that would tear his child to shreds of flesh. The animal blinked, looked away, turned and with one bound disappeared into the tall yellow grass.

Toma lowered himself into his father's arms, buried his face in Joha's chest hairs and was silent. His father's body still rigid with fury, his arm muscles still bulging in preparation to fight, to strangle the animal in defence, remained unresponsive until he could relax and press Toma to himself with a grunt of relief.

He held him tight while collecting his weapon and the skin pouch, then moved cautiously away from the tree to more open country where he could see whether the animal had left.

Toma soon forgot the frightening leopard when they came across a termite mound promising a meal of ants. Joha gave the top a clout with his handaxe at which moment an aardvark shot out of a hole in it and lumbered away. Just as he was going to throw his hunting stick to kill the prey, Joha noticed out of the corner of his eye a mongoose running from the other side where Toma had been waiting and now with a cry of delight was giving chase. It ran towards some bushes and Joha abandoning the kill gave the thicket a suspicious glance and dashed after Toma to catch him before anything else might have a chance. To the disappointment of father and son the termites had long left their mound empty.

At sunset the savannah heat rapidly dissipated and a cool breeze swept across the land that was about to fade into twilight. Joha stopped by a tree, scooped out a depression in the ground with the help of his digging stick while Toma assisted by pushing away loose soil with his hands. Over it they built a temporary shelter with short acacia branches planted in the ground to meet in the middle. The thorny stems would deter animal intruders and a tree always provided a final means of escape if necessary.

When the last segment of red sun sank out of sight it became totally dark apart from starlight and a waning moon. Joha pushed Toma into the shelter, followed through the narrow entrance on hands and knees, shuffled about on the grass they had placed in the hollow to find the most comfortable position, put a protective arm round Toma, and both went to sleep at once. The night was always filled with noises: night birds called to each other, frogs croaked by the river, hyenas howled in the distance, there were snuffles from passing animals in the dark, and predators roared and snarled. Joha was not disturbed by such normal noises but he had dreams that pulled him awake: his family appeared with white faces or he saw unimaginably huge shelters rearing into the sky. Glowing eyes without an animal body but suspended instead on long sticks crossed his dream landscape. Always he woke with a start, bewildered, feeling as though his body was not there under him. Often he was terror-stricken, alone in these nightmares, unable to understand them. The only way he could settle down again was to put an arm over Toma so that he was reassured his child was there as before.

There was one night when it was Toma's turn to wake with a shout. He tossed about, cried out in pain, arms and legs twitching and in his agony hammered for help on Joha with small fists. In the dark it was impossible to see what was the matter. Joha took him on his lap but straight away uttered a yelp, pushed Toma out of the shelter, jumped after him and ran with the screaming child to the river where after a brief glance round in the glimmering starlight, he sat him in a pool of water. Again and again he splashed him until he stopped crying and only then sat next to him to drown the ants tormenting him through his body hair with their cutting pincers for mouthparts, that had so nearly overwhelmed them both in their sleep.

Each dawn Joha obeyed the inner voice that said, 'Go!' but he was mindful to follow a direction that would enable them to return to the river for water at a further point, possibly stalking and clubbing small buhu also come to drink. On one such occasion, Joha, with Toma at his side drinking with cupped hands from the trickle of water in the middle of the riverbed, became aware of some creatures on the other side of the wide flood plain. They looked like members of his family, could they possibly be the company he had longed to meet? Toma, unaware of them, began running about and digging into the soft sand for worms while his father sat motionless, excited inwardly at the prospect of a meeting and a chance to acquire a female.

Those on the far side seemed equally excited, waving their arms in his direction. Joha could just hear the noise they were making, a great din of chatter. A group detached itself from the main horde and moved across the plain towards him and with decreased distance he could see they had pink pendulous breasts, obviously females. The males remaining behind continued their excited waving. Joha stood up, uncertain as to whether he should make some sign of friendliness that might attract a female to his side.

The nearer they came, the more was Joha's unease because although recognisably female, these were squat, slightly bent from the shoulder down, and walked with a ponderous gait, swinging body and arms from side to side. They were not of his family, their big heads heavily jawed, their longer arms and hairier bodies quite unlike any he had seen before. They looked like wild creatures, ugly and repugnant, dashing his hope of meeting and possibly getting a female.

They stopped on the opposite bank and there was a sudden silence. Toma at this moment became aware of them and ran to his father, arms anxiously wound round his legs. This set the females off: they shrieked, they howled, jumped up and down, and extended their hands as if to grasp him. Joha was left in no doubt that they wanted Toma. Astonished, he looked among them, then at the group of males in the distance and realised they had no young.

The females began lumbering across the sandy riverbed, some wildly grasping the air in a frenzy, some showing begging hands, all of them shouting unintelligibly at Toma who was crying and trying to attract his father's attention to lift him.

When the front female was almost upon them Toma let out a howl of fear. Joha snatched up his child, took a leap in the opposite direction and began running across the savannah, hotly pursued. With their heavy bodies and strange way of walking however, the females were no match for his agility. After a while certain he had shaken them off, Joha eased into his loping gait which allowed Toma to let go of his neck and to climb round to his father's back, from where Joha swung him up onto his shoulders. Having forgotten his earlier fright and enjoying his elevated position he shouted, 'There buhu!' any time a hare or antelope broke cover but Joha was in no mood for hunting, shaken by his experience with the begging females. If there were no children among them he understood their need to find some. Why however could they not produce a child as his female had done?

ANOTHER CHILD

Baratu assisted his wife in weeding her garden plot where she grew beans and sweet potatoes between the taller maize plants. He visited his relatives, arranged for a man to mend the leak in his roof, helped the children with homework, took his car to the garage for a new tyre, and spent the rest of his time up in the Museum helping the Lady Archaeologist although he was not meant to be at work.

'You must be with your family,' she insisted.

It occurred to him this was an opportunity to test her understanding. 'But I am with my family, my ancestors are telling me to help you in identifying them.'

She shot him a glance, obviously wondering whether he was joking but he looked her straight in the eye without changing his serious expression.

'I suppose,' she agreed, 'you as an African might have greater claim to calling them your ancestors than I have, but don't forget our DNA is totally similar.'

She had missed his emphasis on the words 'are telling me'. Would she understand if he told her about the voices? No! She would probably pretend to be interested, he knew, but as for 'understanding', well, who would?

Next day she had news for him: he could return to fieldwork with the plane that was taking two visiting geologists to the site. Much relieved that he was going, he gave the children extra pocket money, had sex with his wife that night hoping it would last him for a while, and was packed and ready next morning when the Museum car picked him up to join the scientists for the flight.

Much was made of greeting him. They called him 'the famous fossil finder' and said they looked forward to doing fieldwork in his company. As soon as they were airborne one reached for his briefcase of scientific articles.

After a while he exclaimed, 'Here it is. Baratu, have you heard about that archaeological expedition the Americans and Ethiopians went on in Ethiopia a few years ago? This is an old report of their findings, nevertheless always interesting to read. The article describes the fossils they excavated not that terribly far from your camp as the crow flies. When analysed and dated, they were found to be the remains of near-Homo sapiens eroded from ancient river and beach deposits. Apparently they lived near a lake about 160,000 thousand years before now.'

'Yes, I heard they were almost Homo sapiens.'

'That's what it says.'

'Some people had to revise their ideas,' said the second geologist dryly, and lapsed into silence looking out at the ancient landscape below them reaching to the horizon.

The exchange made Baratu think. Homo erectus was around for thousands of years before now, but according to the books his brain never quite reached the size of that of the Homo sapiens. What sort of people were these in the Ethiopian region? What sort of intelligence did they have? The Lady Archaeologist talked a lot about cranial capacity and increased ability. Every time a prehistoric child was born with an even slightly bigger brain, it might have had a greater chance to escape from danger and when it grew to adulthood would make advantages for itself in food gathering and mating. The offspring might inherit the enhanced ability and so gradually a line of more intelligent beings developed.

He thought of his own children. Were they cleverer than he was? Could their brains be bigger, or were humans at a standstill? The Lady talked of gradual evolution influenced by environmental opportunities. Well, his children were going to have the best education and his wife made sure they had the best food. What more was needed, he wondered, to give them improved intelligence?

— — — — — —

Time was of no meaning in that vast savannah where day dawned regularly with the rising of a red disc sometimes distorted to larger size by the extra clear atmosphere and where it set at an almost visually recognisable speed, large again and glowing with the colour of fresh blood. The moon crossed the night skies in its various sizes, waxing, waning, but not uniform of colour because there were always grey shadows on it. The vegetation greened or dried yellow, water was either abundant or hard to find and Toma grew older, reflecting by his size and body flesh the amount Joha found for them to eat.

Each morning both set out gathering, hunting little animals before these could reach their holes, and avoiding the herds of large grazers that were always accompanied by lions and possibly many other carnivores camouflaged in the grass. A full stomach was success; going to sleep hungry, failure.

Toma, older and fleeter of foot, had become a good little hunter and when they caught sight of an animal camouflaged by a thicket, Joha motioned him to creep round to prevent its escape on the other side. Just as he aimed his throwing stick however, there came the faint sound of distant screams.

Joha stopped aiming and Toma straightened up. The duiker seeing a chance leaped out of the thicket and fled. Both father and son exchanged a glance and Joha began to run, not as fast as he would have wished because Toma couldn't yet keep up but nevertheless at speed towards the source of the noise. It sounded like a child screaming for help, a call that Joha answered without hesitation, feet lightly touching the ground in hunting mode, his son not far behind.

The screaming came in spurts sometimes ceasing all together and then starting up shrilly and becoming louder and desperate. Joha put on an extra sprint leaving Toma further behind, leaped over small rocks and bushes and saw below him in a depression two figures, one smaller than the other, locked in struggle. The smaller must be the one screaming. He took the scene in and with his agility and the strength of his great size ran and leaped down the slope making very little noise by comparison with the howls of the little figure. He took a last jump and brought his fist down in a hammer blow on the head of a large male. It took him but one movement to bring out his cudgel that split the head of the creature already tottering from the impact.

The smaller one stopped screaming, looked up in astonishment, then took a leap towards Joha curling its legs round his middle and hanging on to his chest hairs just as Toma would have done at an earlier time. He dropped the cudgel and stick and held the child to him but suddenly aware that his own life might be in danger picked up his weapons again and hurried up between the rocks to find Toma.

The boy was still running to catch up and when they met, Toma's expression at the sight of his father with the extra burden made Joha loosen its grip gently so that it slid to the ground. It was as tall as Toma, a young female with extraordinarily long black hair and as far as they were concerned a strange face down which the tears were still running while her body was shaken by great sobs that would not cease.

Joha took out some berries he had in his skin pouch and offered them to her but she would not take them. She stood there crying and sobbing hysterically while Joha looked on helpless and wondering what he could do with her. Meanwhile Toma hunted round for something to eat and put some beetles in her hand. She stopped crying, sat down and looked at them with interest. This encouraged Toma to look for more titbits and every time he returned with some tender leaves, a bird's egg he found in a nest hanging from a branch and some more beetles, her tears decreased and her sobs subsided. Finally silent she suddenly lay down on the ground, curled up with her knees towards her chin and went to sleep breathing evenly.

All this time Joha had not only tried to think of what he could do with her but had kept a look out for the family who might be searching for their child. He believed Toma and himself to be in great danger. If they found the stranger - the fuzimo - he had killed they might blame him not only for the killing but also for stealing the child. Fearfully he looked back at the rocks hiding the depression. They might come over them at any moment with throwing sticks poised, aiming to kill him and then would take back their child and Toma. He could not wait to return the child to them and risk Toma's life. No, they must flee and fast.

He picked up the sleeping child without her waking and set out at a pace holding her, head, shoulders and arms dangling the other side of his massive shoulder. It was awkward carrying her when he needed his weapons to be at the ready. Toma held out his hands for them and added them to his own smaller ones. Father and son, with the new addition, made their way at a trot through the bleak and rocky landscape further and further away from the unseen camp from which the marauder must have abducted the child.

The rocky terrain strewn with boulders was firm underfoot where pebbles from a previous river in flood had been left on the reddish soil, allowing them good progress. Joha put his burden down occasionally to rest his shoulder but she remained in a deep sleep, her long hair falling over her strange face. Toma brushed it aside gently, looking questioningly at his father who understood his son was wondering what they would do with her. He had no answer except that he knew she could not be returned to wherever her family might be, neither could she be abandoned any more than he would have left Toma to be eaten by buhu. So he put her back on his shoulder and they moved on in the direction he was always drawn.

When his burden woke and he let her slide down to an upright position, they were subjected to a flow of sounds they had never heard before. She stood before them, a lanky figure with lighter skin than theirs and that dark long hair, gesticulating and telling them something but in an altogether new mode of communication in contrast to Joha's and Toma's meagre daily vocabulary of words. The female spouted many and the sound went up and down accompanied by her pointing and waving of arms and hands as she tried to make them understand. They stood still and perplexed until she finished and looked at them expectantly, and when they still didn't respond she took Joha's hand in a firm manner and tugged at him to walk on. The message was clear: she was anxious to get away from the location.

This female child who had jumped into his arms, this little fuzimo with long legs and long straight black hair, whose utterances Joha could not understand, straightaway changed their lives. Toma's so far had been finding food alongside his father with whom he foraged and hunted, drank water cautiously looking round for dangers, and in watching Joha's ways had learnt how to avoid being attacked by animals. But that was all.

The fuzimo skipped alongside the big male, followed Toma in all his actions, augmented their food by digging up edible tubers they did not know of and filled their lives with her exuberance and gesticulations accompanying a lot of talk they were only beginning to interpret. In the middle of such activity one day Joha called to her, 'Fuzimo!'

She made the 'I hear you' face and stopped digging up a root.

Toma who had been helping her ran up to his father and said, 'No fuzimo, Moogi,' pointing to his playmate. 'Moogi!' he repeated looking at the big male expectantly.

Joha copied him with difficulty. 'Mo-ogi,' he growled in his deep voice and the female immediately came over to him.

Pointing to him jauntily she said, 'Joha,' then putting her hand on her chest pronounced, 'Moogi.'

'Moogi! Moogi, Moogi!' she called in rhythm with her long-legged skip back to digging up the next titbit.

Joha stood watching astonished and forgetting why he had called her. This was a strange little female child.

Moogi's day began with a jump out of the shelter and invariably she managed to find them something to eat, her knowledge of edible plants being truly superior. The bushes around them were in flower and Joha collected them and the leaves but Moogi rooted around and pulled up tender shoots in addition. The pulp of calabashes was a favourite not often found until Moogi seemed to know exactly where to look for them, together with tender leaves and grubs and worms.

Sometimes she collected larger leaves, placed them on the ground and put small pebbles round their edges. Then she took each leaf away, surveyed her work, opened her mouth and made a series of extraordinary sounds while running round her exhibit. The first time this happened Joha and Toma came hurrying and Moogi took Toma's hand urging him to follow her skips. He was soon copying all she did and also learned to laugh but Joha for a while stood still every time he heard his young ones emitting the strange sound until he realised the noise was 'good-good'.

Though Moogi skipped and ran about them in this 'good' manner, Joha could not shake off the moroseness that so often overcame him. All those pleasures he remembered no longer relieved his growing urges, he missed his female and saw no chance of looking for another while his young needed him to guard against predators and to find them enough food.

On one of the day's journeys Joha stopped early when the sun had only just passed the zenith and the shadows were still short. They had reached a place where stones lay around in plenty, of which Joha immediately collected some cores and began hammering one with another. Toma and Moogi watched as he struck the flakes from the dark stone but when he wanted to produce a point at one end his heavy-handed blow with the hammer-stone shattered what he had prepared. He sat looking sadly at the scatter of flakes, noting how he never seemed to be able to work a stone so that it had a cutting edge. His old tools were so blunted by now that he hardly managed to cut flesh from a carcass. How was he going to feed his young? Tearing morsels off with teeth was easy but when it came to carrying flesh he needed to make portions that could be kept in his food pouch.

Toma knew how difficult it was for his father to cut up the buhu they killed or scavenged and he looked on with equal consternation.

Neither noticed Moogi walking up and down turning a stone over here and there and picking some up for closer inspection until she sat down next to Joha with one in each hand.

She gave one of the stones a gentle but sharp tap with the other so that a small flake flew off. Then she turned the stone one quarter way and gave it another light but angled tap. Joha watched with fascination as the child cracked off flake after flake gently but with a sharp ping that rang, whereas his hammering had produced only a dull thud. She moved the worked stone skilfully round until it was of a longish leaf shape with a cutting edge. Toma took it from her and tried cutting a twig on a bush but Joha snatched the tool from him and feeling its sharpness with his big hands placed it in the skin foraging bag. He looked at Moogi with wonder, at a loss for both thought and word but she just laughed at him with that 'good-good' feeling sound and both young began to play by placing a flake on a rock and standing a little distance away, threw their stone missiles to hit the target.

At dawn Joha led his small family through the savannah teeming with herds of grass feeders and their predators. In this open grassland the three moved cautiously, stopping often to let their eyes roam over possible places of ambush. Not only were they afraid of the big cats but also of treacherous wild boars that would suddenly bear down upon them from having hidden in the vegetation ready to attack their legs ferociously as if driven by an inner fury.

As it had rained there was now an abundance of edible flowers visited by insects, roots and tubers plumped out, succulent leaves were everywhere easy food to pick. Toma tried to catch a butterfly, chasing it when it flew low and reaching for it when it whipped upwards out of his reach. His comical and futile efforts made Moogi laugh and Joha who was digging for grubs stopped to listen. His dead female had hardly ever emitted a sound about anything except giving birth, neither could he remember having heard Moogi's sound in his family camp among the young who were always running about play fighting with growls or high-pitched squeals.

Moogi seeing Joha digging took up a dry twig to help him enlarge the hole. She was always helping. Could he possibly leave the gathering to her as the female while he and Toma hunted buhu?

Some time later they noticed a lone small antelope standing in the shade of bushes. Joha motioned to Toma to creep round to stop its escape on the one side while he crouched in the grass and began moving gradually towards it. In their concentration both had forgotten the female.

When Joha thought himself near enough he rose with a leap simultaneously throwing the hunting stick at the throat of the animal. It reared and fell but recovered enough to attempt flight. At that moment Moogi sprang from another side of the bush into its path, flung her arms round its neck and therefore was dragged some paces on. She clung tenaciously, winding her legs round its middle, reached for its small horns and held the head downward so that the animal did a somersault, landing on the ground, Moogi having avoided being under it. At that moment Toma came bounding over tussocks of grass to help her hold the animal until Joha reached them to thrust his second hunting stick into its heart.

He was truly astonished, no female he had known had ever helped in a hunt. Perplexed he looked hard at Moogi's genital area but there was nothing hanging there. She must be a female.

Toma was growing rapidly and Moogi too though she was now the smaller of the two. However when it came to chasing buhu she was in front, outdistancing both males with her slender long legs. It was a game to both Moogi and Toma, their way of competing but Joha was at a loss over her non-female characteristics.

He was no longer as anxious in his watch over his young since the two were always together and the female very alert to danger. Their understanding was complete in the sounds they made to each other of which Joha had learned some words. His way of communication with Toma was still by few words and more body language but when he wanted to talk with the female, Toma helped out by making those fast sounds that still rang unintelligibly in Joha's ears to the latter's immense irritation.

Of course Moogi had come into his life in a strange way and he recognised the fact that she was different, with not a day passing without something new to be noticed about her. Lately she had started to look at him in a way that was unnerving. He remembered the look in females' eyes when they offered themselves for copulation. It had excited him sexually and it did now. But Moogi was his child, he must control himself, she was not for mating. The more she awoke his desires, the greater was his search to find another camp, to find that crowd of females of which he dreamed when he was not having his nightmares.

No sooner had the sun risen than he wanted to be off, following his subconscious direction finder unquestioningly through the plains, past giant baobab trees and through forest islands of plodding elephants and top-grazing giraffes but so far there had been no sighting of another group of fuzimo.

POISON

Baratu was resting his feet. He had shown the two geologists round the area until they saw what seemed to be an ancient lakeshore. They were getting out their geology hammers when he left them to explore, glad to get away from scientific talk.

He had on the new shoes he had bought on his last visit home and they were pinching his toes in the heat. He took them off and decided to carry them. How those ancestors of his, hominins and more recent ones too would gape at such footwear. Of course, his immediate tribal ancestors had used car tyres and made sandals out of the flat part with thongs of cowhide to hold them on the feet. He himself remembered walking to school barefoot which was so much cooler than the confining leather. When within sight of the building he had put his shoes on again.

He got up from the hot ground and prepared to examine his intended path for signs of fossils. The Lady Archaeologist was due next week, having previously warned them that the team must work to find her some new bones or they might all be threatened with closure of the site.

Stepping lightly, his wide feet hardly leaving an impression on the pebbly ground, he found himself marching to a rhythm. The sound of singing coming from somewhere far off reached his ears, repetitive, with a sort of beat, and he had responded without being aware of doing so.

He screwed up his eyes in the sun's glare to look into the distance, suddenly worried that it could be a band of cattle thieves on their way south to the rich tribal lands of the area. Breaking into song was usually associated with agricultural work, but here on the border with another territory there might be different customs. Not a speck of dust showed on the horizon; nobody was in sight.

After a while there was the same rhythm again, very faint but nevertheless a song. Puzzled, he turned slowly about himself, then cocked his head to one side towards the noise but still saw nothing.

What connection could there be between taking off his shoes and the singing?

It was very hot, and taking off his shoes made him realise he could strip off his shirt, after all there was no one to see him. He smiled at a memory of himself as a young child when he never wore one.

To his astonishment the rhythm became more audible, definitely a woman singing and with a lilt that was soothing. He could feel it relaxing him.

A thought struck: shoes off, shirt off, not far off being almost naked. No, he was not going to take off his shorts as well to be as bare as the hominins must have been. That's who it was. Them.

Suddenly he was frightened. Would they really get more in contact if he seemed like them? In his worry he began to walk back to camp fast, hurrying without another look as though somebody was after him. Returning early he found it empty, the fossil team also out looking for new sites.

With time on his hands he began to wonder whether it was hominins or present day humans he had heard. 'You must have been happy, singing as you walked,' he greeted the returning fossil team.

'Baratu, we worked hard today, walking for miles examining the ground, and in silence. What were you hearing, cattle thieves?'

He nodded. 'Maybe.' Let them think he had. So it must have been his ancestors after all, trying to contact him, and how had he responded? Instead of searching the area for their fossils he had turned back. Now he could not remember the spot: everywhere looked the same in that terrain unless one left a marker. He would try and retrace his steps tomorrow.

'Sorry,' he said, speaking to himself but addressing them.

— — — — — —

The three wanderers walked from dawn to dusk, Joha's way of following the urge to go although he did not know where, nor could he have explained why. Toma, accustomed to the daily journey, knew no different lifestyle and Moogi tagged along happily. On the way everything was interesting to the two: the collecting and eating of food, finding of water, and the life of animals all around them, feeding, breeding, fighting, dying. The threesome family kept their distance as they watched the munching, bone-cracking beasts feasting on each other. Nearer, Toma and Moogi examined everything that crawled, dug, flew and swam, and attempted to catch fish with their hands and hunting sticks but hardly ever successfully. Frogs and toads were easy prey along the river banks: a knock on the head and they could be eaten limb by limb.

Excited chirps meant a bird was defending its eggs or fledglings against a predator and thereby giving away its position. Therefore when they heard chirruping, Toma rushed ahead in fun to be the first to raid the nest, but coming up against a tall bush, he heard a commotion beyond and instead of going round to see, he wanted to waste no time, parted some twigs and looked through. A snake was in skirmish with a small furry animal. It darted hither and thither looking for an advantageous position from which to bite while the snake curved and coiled this way and that, keeping its neck out of the way but trying to find the opportunity to sink its fangs. As fast as lightning the snake reared back and up to strike but the animal streaked sideways out of its sight, and with Toma's face the nearest foreign object, the snake ejected a stream of poison which sprayed on the leaves around him and also in his eyes. He yelled with the sudden stabs of pain and stumbled backwards. Moogi who had just reached the side of the bush threw her cudgel at the rearing neck. Too late, even though the snake fell dead on the spot. Of the furry animal there was no sign.

Toma, head in hands, was trembling, eyes screwed up in agony as Joha came running up. He wiped the venom off his son's face with leaves and tried to look at his eyes that Toma could not open because of the pain. The river being some distance off they persuaded him to take their hands and led him slowly to its banks. After a quick inspection to see that the place was safe they splashed him with water, tried to get him to open his eyes and eventually made him lie in the water so he could let the flow run over his closed lids.

Joha made camp a little distance off. Moogi led Toma inside the hastily constructed shelter for a rest on the fresh soft grass they had collected to let him feel safe so that he might calm down. Then Moogi did something Joha had never heard before. She began crooning in a low voice that rose gradually in sound, rolling up and down in a repetitive way. Toma stopped groaning to listen and presently fell asleep. The other two looked at each other, relieved. Exhausted by anxiety over Toma's condition Moogi snuggled into Joha's embracing arms and both were immediately asleep too.

It was very many dawns before a glimmer of sight returned to Toma's eyes. Meanwhile Moogi led him round bushes, trees and rocks, kept up a commentary on the terrain and everything he had to mind, and fed him titbits picked up along the way. She urged Joha to stay near the river to which they could return all the time for her to splash water on Toma's eyes and for him not to suffer thirst as they sometimes did.

Joha made a daily effort to kill a small animal for feeding Toma with fresh flesh. Before long he managed to open his eyes slightly when the extreme pain ceased though he still could not see well and had to be led. Moogi's concentration on helping him vexed Joha. Before the accident he had enjoyed her admiration of his hunting skills, so much so that he was chasing more game and taking pride in showing off how quickly he could catch and kill his prey.

The sight of Moogi's rounded buttocks and developing breasts increasingly affected him and when he stole a glance at them he had to turn away so that neither she nor Toma would see the effect on his ora. He knew his desires were urgent and that he must find a female quickly. Until then he would let Moogi arouse the excitement that gave him pleasure even if he had to keep his distance in regard to sex by remembering she was his child.

Toma's condition, which took up all Moogi's attention, affected her relationship with Joha. Where she had previously smiled admiringly at him she now hardly looked in his direction. Instead of hugging him spontaneously as she had always done, her arms were more often round Toma encouraging him to wade through a river of slippery pebbles or muddy ground after a rainfall. Joha began to suspect that Toma could see perfectly well again and was perhaps faking partial blindness to retain her constant help. It made him wonder what he could do to stop what he took to be his son's game. Take him somewhere far off and leave him to find his way back by reading footprints? That would be a test. Tell Moogi off and stop her from assisting Toma? Give him no more food and demand he take part in hunting? All these ideas ran through Joha's mind as he felt more and more envious of his son and the attention he received from Moogi.

When the inner voice urged a faster pace and Toma could not be persuaded to get a move on, Joha considered abandoning his son to the hyenas. A hit on the head... But every time the thought crossed his mind Joha saw and felt again little Toma the toddler, hands round his neck and trembling. He had protected his son then, how could he do away with him now? And there was Moogi; he wanted those admiring glances of hers. He wanted her altogether as a female and he knew she would not have him if he harmed Toma.

Unable to express his increasing impatience Joha became morose instead, snarling often at his young over nothing, refusing to join in their conversation and eventually making little effort to hunt even small flesh that ran across their way. Worried that they were walking too slowly he jogged thereby making progress difficult for Toma who then had to hold tightly on to Moogi's hand so he would not fall over obstacles. When they slowed down Joha did not and Moogi had to read his tracks to catch up. Neither of the young understood what was going on but feeling rejected, they turned all the more to each other in conversation and laughter until Joha became even more irritable.

His desire to mate and his self-denial where Moogi was concerned spurred him to keep looking for tracks of fuzimo. When the other two found him bent, staring at the ground and asked what was the matter, Joha grunted unintelligibly. His great size and seniority made them respectful of him so that they never questioned his actions.

Joha, concerned with his problems, did not even notice when his son once more joined in foraging and eventually began to vie again with Moogi in the catching of rats, hares, small coloured lizards, and the giant variety marked with camouflaging dark patterns. The three were able to increase their pace and Joha forgetting all previous dark thoughts was satisfied with their marches.

As the two young ones grew taller and stronger it was left to Moogi's skilled hands to make handaxes while Toma provided hunting sticks and cudgels when they became broken. Joha often renewed their skin food pouches which quickly became dry, stiff and unwieldy. When porcupines dropped some of their quills Moogi picked them up and used the sharp end for digging out thorns in her fingers, but having found them not strong enough to skewer chunks of flesh, she learned to whittle pointed sticks instead and sucked the flesh she spiked onto them as she walked along, soon copied by Toma and Joha.

Once again the three were at peace with each other. The young put their energy into keeping up with Joha's easy lope and Joha listened to his inner voice and its directions.

They had gone uphill and down when he indicated a shady tree and Moogi and Toma flung their belongings on the meagre grass, glad of a rest. All around them was empty and quiet in the after-midday heat, the hottest of the day, until a buzzing started up above in the branches. A few insects flew round them but they took no notice. Suddenly the insects swarmed, a ball of bees concentrated above each head and then they attacked, settling and stinging. Arms flailed, legs kicked, and Moogi shouted, 'River!' This was no longer near except that a far-off line of green vegetation indicated water.

The three began to run pursued by the insects like a cloud streaming out behind them. The savannah offered no shelter, no crevices, holes or bushes to hide in. The insects did not leave off: they seemed to sense the hopelessness of their victims' situation and pushed their stings into the soft flesh of the three with vengeance. Pain once more overwhelmed Toma and he began to flag. Joha being taller and bigger attracted even more of the insects than the other two and he too began to slow the breakneck speed, his lungs pumping air until he could not get enough of it and could only manage a jog. Moogi ran on determined not to let the insects kill her. She kept waving the others on with her arms, too frightened to open her mouth to call out. Ahead was a dip in the ground into which she disappeared from their sight. Next moment she was back, hands over her mouth for safety and screaming, 'Water, water!' Frantically she waved to them to run towards her.

There was a muddy watering hole in the depression showing signs of frequent use by animals whose dung lay everywhere. The three threw themselves into the shallow pool and wallowed like hippos until covered in a black stinking mess. The insects gave a last angry hum and retreated, leaving hundreds falling off their victims and dying with cloying mud on their wings. Joha broke off a twig and killed any he found alive by swatting them with the leaves. Moogi and Toma wiped themselves with grass and began pulling the stings from their bodies but it was difficult to see Joha's because of his thick body hair.

'Me go river. They come back,' he announced and jogged off followed by the others still besmeared by stink and worried that they were as yet too near the killer bees. Not until they had reached the river, washed all their stings off and seen no sign of any more of the insects did they feel safe, though shaken by the narrow escape.

Joha made camp early because their bodies were so sore that they could not walk fast. Toma was the one who seemed most affected. He complained incessantly of the pain where the other two lay still and tried to sleep. At dawn Joha made ready to go and reconnoitre the presence of bees since they had to retrieve their belongings but Toma lay moaning incoherently, his face completely swollen. They took him to the river again and Moogi spent the day splashing him with water, while Joha managed to get their things back having found the bees had swarmed.

It seemed that Toma's experience with the spitting snake and now with the deadly bees had taken his spirits away. He was morose, unsmiling. Not even Moogi could cheer him by offering some sweet berries.

Once again Joha became impatient with his son. His inner voice was urging hurry because of the delay but Toma refused to budge from camp.

Moogi as before took care of him and noticed Joha's displeasure. Something had to be done she decided. If only Toma would start walking all would be well again.

On the fourth dawn Moogi emerged from the shelter, picked up her weapons and food pouch, stuck her head back inside and announced, 'Me go.'

'You go?' came the chorus from the other two.

'Me go, no come back.'

Joha was out fast and he too picked up his things. 'Me go, no come back,' he said, copying her tone.

They began walking away. Reaching a vantage point, a low hill, they looked back at the camp to see Toma setting out to follow them. When he caught up, Joha and Moogi looked at each other and by unspoken agreement made no remark. Together they continued on their way as though nothing had happened.

FLOOD

Next day early in the morning while it was still relatively cool, Baratu accompanied the geologists. They discussed the terrain, pointing out where lava had flowed, where silts had piled up and now the elements were eroding them down.

'As we thought, this is the site of an ancient lake. Look at the raised beach,' said one.

'And clear signs of a flood plain and the river that would have brought masses of water during one of the wetter periods when hominins walked this land,' said the other.

Baratu left them to their scientific talk and continued his walk in the hope of finding the spot where he had rested his sore feet.

The cooler air soon heated up to remind him of how it had made him take off his shoes and shirt on the previous day. He would try the same if he found the place where he had heard the singing.

Nothing in the landscape gave him a clue of where he had stood. Nothing moved except the sun, as he noticed by the length of his shadow and the time on his wristwatch. The tufts of dried grass dotted about looked similar, pebbles strewn around made random patterns as they did whenever he looked at them.

An empty day, no finds, was what all the fossil hunters had to contend with. Not to become dejected was one of the most difficult aspects of their work, not to give up.

After hours of trudging over the previous day's terrain, it struck him that he was being punished. Yes, that was it. His ancestors had called him yesterday and he had not responded. That was why he could not find the place again. They were probably causing him to bypass it.

He stopped in his tracks, turned in the direction where he imagined the singing had taken place and called out in his own tribal language.

'Great fathers and mothers, it is good that you let me hear your talk and your singing. I will not have a deaf ear for you next time.'

Satisfied he had propitiated them, he continued back to camp where the other men were waiting with the news that they had made a find that morning.

'We've dug up part of an animal skull. Huge. You had better come and see.'

They spent next day at the site, digging out more bits of skeleton , and after transporting the material by combined effort to the camp, started chipping at the matrix surrounding the fossilised bones.

That evening in the work tent at the long wooden table kept for assembling finds, applying resin to stop bone from falling apart, and working on labelling and packing, the fossil team and the geologists examined their finds in detail. They agreed it was hippo, very large and bearing some cut marks.

Baratu informed the Lady Archaeologist of this discovery on the radiophone.

'I'm coming,' she exclaimed. 'Am due anyhow as I want to see this ancient lakeshore the geologists are exploring.'

'A very important find,' she told them on arrival and after a close look at the fossils. 'Such marks have been reported from elsewhere as well and possibly provide confirmation of hominins doing some butchering. We'll have them examined under magnification. I doubt that they hunted these large animals but they probably cut one up if found dead or injured.'

Possibly and probably, thought Baratu. Could scientists ever leave these words out?

– – – – – –

Joha always chose his night stops carefully: away from a river, spring or waterhole and its animal visitors but if possible near enough to get a drink. A favoured site was one with a tree, so that flesh caught during the day or scavenged from a carcass could be hung from it. The food was cut into strips suspended from thongs or bark fibre that leopards, cheetahs and civet cats could not steal by climbing the tree, and hyenas, wild dogs and jackals failed to reach by jumping up on their hind legs to gain height. Though as had happened before, there was always one animal more agile than the rest who managed to become a thief.

It was important to camp where there were no telltale signs of ants or bees and no holes where snakes or scorpions might be lurking. Furthermore the family always made sure there were no traces of a predator's lair, indicated by droppings or hair caught on a thorn, or remains of horn and hoof indigestible even to vultures and hyenas.

The entrance to the nightly shelter was crucial, opening away from any water source, animal trail and prevailing wind. Toma had learned this lore from his father and though he too helped to decide the location of the camp, Joha's decision was final.

One late day, the sun low, Toma and Moogi became anxious because Joha strode on and on, always restless and never footsore while they were flagging behind. Was he still looking for a suitable camping place? In their opinion they had passed many. Occasionally he searched the sky, took quick intakes of air through his nose, noted the direction of bird flight and bent low to listen to the scuttling of small creatures in the grass. He stopped at the river they were following, found a place where the water spilled over a rocky outcrop, watched the volume and listened intently to the splashing and gurgling. He was obviously troubled but when they asked him what was the matter he remained silent.

On they marched, falling in with Joha's occasional easy lope and stopping when he halted to listen but hearing nothing except for the rustle of leaves and waving of grass blades in the late evening wind. Finally when it was almost dark he led them up a slight rise and put his food pouch down at the top, always a sign that he meant to rest. The night having descended, they pulled up the nearest tufts of grass and bedded down so tired that they slept immediately.

At sunrise Moogi and Toma shared a wild melon picked the previous day, took hold of the grubbing and hunting sticks and were ready to go. Joha who had eaten a few morsels of leftover antelope flesh, to their surprise said an emphatic, 'No!' The two then started looking about for a fuller meal, wandering off down the rise, leaving Joha to build a more substantial shelter. He collected branches from nearby bushes, pushed them hard into the soil along the outer line of an arbitrary oval and bent the upper green twigs to interlace, adding bundles of grass and reeds growing on the river's edge. With another glance at the sky he scraped a little runnel round the shelter with a run-off furrow, using a sharpened stick. The work lasted some time: the young having grown taller, the shelters had to grow with them and now took longer to construct.

Activity made him hungry. Where were Moogi and Toma? Somewhere near collecting food surely? He walked down and round the rise of the campsite but could not find them. He retraced his steps, looked into the distance from the top of the rise but there was no sign of them either, as far as he could see. Down he went again looking for their footprints and began tracking through the grass, imagining they must be somewhere near and just to make sure, called their names loudly in case they had gone to the river further upstream or down. Silence set in after his shout when all creatures about him stopped their own calling. Suddenly misgiving rose in his mind. At all times the three of them were never far from each other because of an unspoken rule resulting from the constant danger from flesh-eating animals. Their absence was worrying. Joha began trotting, following the easy-to-read track of his young.

Why were they not coming into sight? Why had they gone so far? After some time the grass gave way to a pebble-strewn flood plain where their footprints were difficult to read except by dislodged stones and occasionally there were imprints of toes in an area of sandy soil. The sun rose to its zenith, the heat began to make the air shimmer, his hunger urged him to stop and find food, and thirst turned his eyes longingly to where the far band of trees indicated water. Instead he hurried on only hampered by having to read the track more carefully.

By now his fear was fuelled by his inability to understand what was happening. The young, supposedly foraging for food, had walked an unnecessary distance judging by the growth of tubers his cutting of branches had revealed round the bottom of the rise. Joha remembered those strange females at the riverbed stretching out their hands beseechingly for his Toma child, and what about the incident when that male had captured the screaming Moogi. His flood of memory dug even deeper to the day of his search for the female and Toma, and the hopelessness of that situation and his despair at that time. The feeling of it crept back into his being, making him fearful of what he might find ahead.

On he went, sometimes finding the track with ease, sometimes almost losing it, so that he walked bent over not to miss the slightest clue. Joha became even more worried. What if he did not find them – before it was dark? What would he do? There was not only a general silence everywhere, but also an absence of animals. With nightfall they would surely be prowling to kill.

Going up a rise, feet had trodden down dry grass. Following the trail he reached the top. Below him on the flanks of an ant heap sat Moogi and Toma with their backs to him. He stopped with relief followed by an anger that made him creep round silently through the acacia scrub to confront them. They jumped up joyfully and ran to him, each taking one of his hands. Joha who moments before had felt so angry that he had an urge to wield a club, became confused by his emotions: relief, retaliation for making him so anxious, desire to hurt, then happiness and above all, puzzlement.

His lack of words in Moogi's language in which Toma was now so fluent, caused him difficulties when formulating questions, but he did not need to ask any because she burst into one of her floods of sounds. She had found a track of footprints possibly female. Could it be a fuzimo? They had followed but had just lost the trail. She waved her arms in this and that direction, excited, eyes shining, tugging at him to gain his full attention. Toma nodded and repeated her words in emphasis and then started again in the form of communication his father understood. Was this not what he was looking for, a female?

Joha stood torn with the desire to follow the trail, perhaps finding the prize he had so longed for. An anxious look at the sky urged a return to camp. No, this was not the moment to search for the possible meeting with a female fuzimo.

'We go camp,' he told them. 'Fuzimo run far.'

Toma and Moogi, disappointed by his decision, started complaining of hunger but Joha refused to stop to forage. Suddenly he swung his cudgel at their ant heap, sending clods flying and revealing termites scurrying all over them.

The three picked up the clods and licked them off, glad of a partial meal after all.

During the night the rains came. Joha slept fitfully under steady drips through the dry thatch. He dreamed of chasing some flesh but suddenly found himself in a blaze of light that made it impossible to see from where it came. Strange voices were shouting strange words, he was surrounded. Panic-stricken he made a dash for it and broke through but the strangers pursued him. He heard the loud clatter of feet and then sharp cracks of noises that went right through him. Making a last effort to escape he reared up to find it was daylight and he was very wet. Toma and Moogi lay huddled together sound asleep despite the water seeping from under them.

He emerged from the shelter, finding the dark sky lit up by flash after flash of lightning followed by the cracks of thunder that had woken him. Then he straightened up with astonishment, looking at an extraordinary sight. His guesses had been right about all the previous day's smells, sights and sounds promising a rainstorm but he could not understand how a lake had formed so quickly all around. The river was in flood, its course no longer visible but indicated by a line of half-submerged trees. Their rise was now an island, muddy water gushing past and the further shore very far away. They were totally cut off.

Toma and Moogi crept out of the shelter and exclaimed in fright so that he put his arms round them reassuringly. Their plight became obvious soon enough when they ate the food they had found the day before, realising there could not be much more on their bit of ground. The tuber plants Joha had noticed growing round their hill were now under water.

The day was spent sitting at the edge of the flood, Toma and Moogi cooling their feet in the muddy water, and Joha anxiously watching the imperceptibly rising level that made them move further and further up towards the shelter. He regretted having had to choose the slightly elevated campsite hastily and without a tree that might now save their lives if the waters overwhelmed them.

They drank the brown liquid, finished the few remaining leaves in the food pouch and settled down to watch things floating downriver. There were uprooted bushes and trees, and animal carcasses swelling in the sun's increasing heat so that their legs turned stiffly towards the sky. Those still alive tried to keep their heads above water but were drowning nevertheless. Crocodiles tried to swim towards the prey but were being swept along like the rest by the swift flow of water.

Everything was too far out midstream for the three to catch any of the buhu to kill or pick for flesh, and even hippos that usually preferred the edge of rivers and lakes so that they could graze and wallow in shallow water were being pushed at the current's speed and were wild-eyed with fright.

At nightfall Joha pulled up what remained of grass on the little hill and wove the bundles between the twigs of the thin branches forming the shelter. He remained outside to keep watch over the rising water lit up by a brilliant display of sheet and fork lightning on the horizon. Moogi and Toma lying side by side for warmth were bedded on damp grass inside, knowing Joha kept watch. Thunder rolled towards the location nearer and nearer, the wind got up tearing bits of grass from the shelter, and it began to pour, lashing Joha's face.

At dawn the young were up as well, wet and hungry, digging for anything they could find on the small amount of ground the waters allowed them. Carcasses were still floating by but none landed on the edge of the flood. Joha felt desperate, not only because of the hunger his young must be suffering too but also because he did not know what to do. The rain set in on and off and they sat close together in the water running off their rise. The young dozed, Joha slept intermittently tired out from watching the flood during the night, but though the water seemingly had stopped rising, it showed no sign of subsiding.

That night Moogi and Toma did not go to the dripping wet shelter from which they had plucked all the edible leaves. They remained huddled up to Joha, one on each side of his big body, their heads meeting in his generous lap. Dawn revealed vultures sitting on all the tops of trees showing above the flood. They fluttered down noisily onto any carcass floating by, pushing each other off dangerously near the surface of the water yet managing to hover and fly alongside the dead buhu.

Moogi left her companions, saying she would sit right by the water's edge to try catching anything that came past.

After a while she waded into the water, further and further up to her chin. When Joha realised the danger she was in, he jumped into the flood and was desperately reaching out to her when the force of the current suddenly carried her away. He remained staring after her bobbing head. He could not swim. Returning to the island, father and son stood side by side looking with horror at the place in the flood where she had been moments before, until Toma hid his face in his hands unable to face the calamity.

It was unbelievable! She had been sitting there, next moment gone. The water was gushing past noisily, carrying crocodiles and hippos in the same direction in which she had disappeared. Surely she must have been killed at once? Tears rolled down Toma's face mingling with the rain and for once Joha did not console him but stood forlorn, staring at the flood with a stupefied expression. The rain increased, the water ran down the rise and made rivulets round them but the two figures didn't stir. Although it was only midday, heavy clouds darkened the sky giving the landscape a look of evening.

Joha coming to after a while looked at his son sideways, wondering how he could find food for him. Toma was all he had left now that Moogi too must have met her death. Once more he waded into the flood, hunting sticks and cudgel ready, staring at the muddy eddies in the hope of killing something they could eat.

His concentration was interrupted by the movement of a figure on the opposite bank. There was Moogi waving arms and jumping up and down to attract their attention. Her action was in typical Moogi style. Joha bellowed a response that rang across the water, while Toma wildly gesticulating shouted her name. Having revealed her whereabouts she turned away and began foraging, bending and straightening to gather food. They were stunned with astonishment and overjoyed with relief, although neither could understand the situation. How could it be that Moogi was alive and walking about on the other side of the flood? They watched and watched until she disappeared from view behind vegetation. Moogi was alive but they were no nearer getting food.

Although they continued glancing at the further shore she did not appear again. Joha began worrying about her safety because despite being a good hunter she had no hunting stick with which to defend herself, and though she was a fast runner some buhu could outdistance her unless she climbed a tree. Looking all along the opposite shore there was not one to be seen.

Joha could not keep still. He wondered why Moogi had disappeared from view. What could she be doing except foraging, and he constantly rose to search for her figure through the gloom of the dark day quickly changing into night. The rain stopped, gradually stars emerged and a full moon broke through the remaining cloud cover, bathing the floodwater and the landscape in luminosity.

While Toma lay huddled on the damp ground trying to sleep, Joha stood not to miss a passing carcass and occasionally looked across for a sign of Moogi. From time to time he took a drink to stop his gnawing hunger but otherwise stood still, hunting stick in hand, watching, determined not to let Toma starve to death. As his gaze tried to penetrate the dark for anything alive floating by, he saw something black some distance away and tensing his muscles made ready to throw the stick should it turn into an animal close enough to reach. The dark round shape was coming swiftly, visible against the water's reflection. His hope rose, surely this was going to be a certain kill? He was ready, hunting stick poised. Suddenly the animal reared out of the water at which moment the shape became familiar just in time to stop him from throwing his weapon at what turned into the figure of Moogi. She waded across to him laden with the food pouch she had taken with her thrown over a shoulder. He helped her ashore where she keeled over exhausted and lay in the moonlight, her long hair draped over her face looking almost dead.

'Moogi!' Joha kept saying. 'Moogi!' and he swept her hair to one side and picked her up to cradle her, holding her shivering body to him.

At dawn Toma awoke to find Joha still sitting holding Moogi in his arms, both asleep. Beside them the open food pouch indicated they had eaten but had left plenty for him and he lost no time to feed.

When everybody was up Moogi told him in her words and gesturing what had happened and Toma translated where his father could not understand. She had been swept away with the current round a bend to the opposite shore. She spent her time gathering food, always going upstream. When darkness set in she went into the water, believing herself safe because she had observed crocodiles getting plenty to eat. The flood carried her downstream until she struck out swimming to get across to the campsite.

Father and son looked at her with admiration and at the pouch that still held plenty more to eat, though they wondered how much longer they would have to wait until they could all three forage on the opposite shore.

It was not just the flood that was worrying but the weather as well. It poured down, stopped, the sun appeared briefly to dry them off, only for them to be drenched again by another lot of rain. The enforced inactivity was boring and depressing with no let-up in sight.

Day after day drowned animals floated past, and day after day the water crept up almost imperceptibly until they found themselves sitting in it and having to move up the very last section of the rise. The food pouch lay empty, their bit of ground had no more to offer and the carcasses never floated near enough to be hauled in. Joha mostly looked into the distance where his inner direction finder told him he should be, and all three sat huddled together, a sad little group on a tip of ground showing above a vast brown lake.

Time passed, dawn followed dawn, Joha felt to blame for not choosing a rise with a tree, Moogi and Toma dozed with hunger. Vultures continued circling and by now had to find a perch on the last top branches of submerged trees. Every so often one of the three humans moved to fill their gnawing stomach with a drink. Joha tore at the stiff skin food pouches and they tried chewing pieces from them but their strength was almost gone. Looking at the plight of the other two he wondered what more he could do? He closed his eyes frequently, resigned to die.

In their misery they did not realise the floodwater was rising again until it was all around them where they sat and soon past their knees standing up. Their ground was now underwater. Joha became wild-eyed with panic and Toma glancing at Moogi, so much shorter, saw the water was fast reaching up to her buttocks. When Joha next looked round she was gone.

'Moogi!' he bellowed and, 'Moogi!' they both shouted, again and again, their voices trembling in desperation. The roaring of the increased volume of flood prevented them from hearing even if she could have answered.

The water rose further. As Toma was almost as tall as his father both were now submerged up to their waists, and Joha in his panic continued to bellow. So much so that they missed seeing Moogi appear behind them on the edge of what had been their island. When they noticed her, she was struggling to tug the swollen carcass of an antelope by its tail. Finally succeeding to manoeuvre it alongside the males she told them to hold on to its legs and to push it back into deeper water. Joha totally astonished and panic stricken would not kick away from the ground no matter how much she shouted instructions. At that moment another volume of water flowing downstream lifted his legs off and took the buoyant carcass along without Moogi having to exert herself any further. Toma who always listened to her, did as told and made sure his father's hands stayed holding one of the animal's horns.

Their journey was over before Joha had time to think. The swollen float was lifted downstream towards the further shore where the waters were deflected by a group of rocks, and they trod ground. Walking ashore Joha regained his composure and when Moogi flopped down exhausted, carried her to safety.

Toma asked her how she had found the carcass to save them. She was watching the dead buhu floating by, she said. On one of them there was an animal with its forelimbs on the carcass and therefore its head out of water. It was still alive. There were no more crocodiles she had noticed too. When the flood started creeping up on their bit of ground she realised they were going to drown, so she went into the water to find a carcass.

'I see dead buhu. I push, I push to you,' she explained.

Joha looked at her closely. What a strange female this was, always helping them and now helping them not to die. He put out his arms and she leaned forward to receive his big hug of thankfulness. He held her, aware of her breasts against his chest and feeling he did not want to let her go. She yielded and responded by putting her arms round his massive neck.

Toma, looking at the two, decided they needed food. All their possessions were lost: food pouches, hunting sticks, cudgels and Moogi's stone axes, but there was a harvest of mushrooms growing all around, sprung up during the periods of damp followed by hot sunshine. A dead hippo was lying near the water's edge. Toma picked up two pebbles, clashed them together and using the resulting flakes, hacked pieces of flesh from it, then cracked open a long bone to see if there was any marrow.

They sat in the pouring rain, greedily feeding on the food he had gathered.

VIOLENCE

On her next visit the Lady Archaeologist showed Baratu a rough sketch made by the geologists of the ancient lakeshore.

'I want to have a walk along all this.' She traced a finger round the hatched shore on the paper. 'Baratu, ask a few men to come with us, will you?'

He arranged for two of the most experienced men to accompany them; the rest of the team were to continue their dig for hippo fossils.

The four of them spread out in a line abreast, each about two metres from the next, each intent on making a surface find or marking a spot worth further investigation.

Suddenly Baratu became aware of another person or a sound. Somebody talking? It must be persons far off because the fossil team were walking in silence at that moment.

'Stop! Someone is following,' he said quietly and they immediately closed ranks. Bandits had been seen in the area by the pilot coming in to land the last consignment. There were always thieves about looking for food and money and a quick getaway where nobody could catch them in the vast arid region.

'Keep together and let's have a quick look around,' commanded the Lady Archaeologist. They searched the immediate vicinity without finding a clue.

She looked enquiringly at Baratu. 'What did you actually hear?'

'I'm not sure. Perhaps it was in my mind.'

She looked at him thoughtfully. 'And now?'

He shook his head.

She asked the others to be absolutely quiet. Baratu was to walk around and stop if he heard anything again. He retraced his steps to where they had been walking and marched up and down. 'Here.'

'Good! We will dig a trial trench at this spot,' she said. 'We know Baratu finds a lot of fossils. I'm beginning to think he is like certain people in

England who can find water with wands,' and she told them of the age-old custom of using twigs or metal rods to divine the presence of water.

'What has water to do with a bandit?' asked one of the men.

The Lady Archaeologist chose not to hear the question as she went to find a stick with which to score the ground for the proposed trench. She measured off a metre by a metre, took a compass bearing, marked the spot on the geologists' temporary map and told the men to leave a cairn of stones for their return next day with digging tools.

When he recalled the conversation about finding water and his suspicion of somebody following them, Baratu also could not make the connection but knowing the Lady Archaeologist was very clever, he trusted she knew what she was talking about.

On the following day, shovels, trowels and brushes followed pickaxes, and when the first Stone Age handaxe came to light, the Lady Archaeologist gave Baratu, digging near her, a hug of excitement. Some of the axes seemed to have been discarded before being finished, the flakes still lying near as the team dug everything up and admired the workmanship.

One of the team turned to the Lady asking, 'When you mentioned water diviners yesterday, what have they to do with this find?'

'When Baratu heard or more likely felt the presence of a person or people,' she explained, 'I thought of the English water diviners. Of course we don't know whether Baratu's divination talent responds to the water that was here to supply the needs of ancient people, or just to the ancient hominins, or both.'

— — — — — —

After the flood had subsided, the land bloomed all around. There were always seeds in the ground dormant until rain allowed them to shoot almost overnight. The flood plain dried out gradually; remaining pools contained frogs and even fish left behind, unable to get back to the river channel somewhat altered by new sandbanks. The scrub of acacia bloomed yellow with flowers, tamarind trees grew their edible long pods, gourds greened and then turned yellow and hard. After a while there were seeds and nuts as a tasty extra.

Joha, Moogi and Toma suddenly had no need to hunt or forage, no need to safari on, which was fortunate because Moogi was so exhausted that she could hardly raise herself to eat. She lay in the sun most of the time now that the rains had ceased and slept. Joha or Toma had to stand guard and therefore neither ventured far. This situation was trying because they had become used to marching all day, foraging as they went.

Soon all three regained their vigour and began replacing weapons, tools and bags. Moogi surrounded herself with stone cores, chose one as a hammer and each day practised making handaxes, sharp-edged all round and lozenge-shaped, one for each of them. As usual Joha watched her dexterity with admiration and envy. Using his new one and some discarded sharp flakes, he whittled sticks from the straightest branches he could find and left them to dry before trying them for strength. As it was almost impossible to find straight wood, the throwing sticks were fairly short and the cudgels even shorter when he could make one from the thickening of wood at the junction of branches. Like the shaping of stone, the cutting of green wood and peeling away the bark was hard work. That was why the loss of their tools and weapons was such a calamity.

The sharp flakes were also useful for scraping the edible pulp out of gourds. The outer rinds of this type of pumpkin lay about the camp drying, until one day Moogi scraped the inside of a whole one clean and fetched water in it from the river. Joha and Toma immediately copied her and used their vessels for drinking. When they found some already hollow because the pulp had withered away, they cut the very top of the more slender necks, tied a thong round and carried water in them.

Many carcasses had been left high and dry on the sandbanks by the receding floodwaters so that for a while the three were surrounded day and night by animals. Hyenas, wild dogs, lions and vultures gorged themselves on meat and bone to the accompaniment of snarls, yelps and screeches as each lot had to await its turn in the hierarchy of meat eaters. Even cheetahs and leopards which normally preferred to hunt fresh meat were tempted to snatch a bite from animals only recently dead. At first, Joha had been able to get some flesh for their own consumption but with the arrival of so many buhu it became too dangerous to join in the scavenging.

After some days of the bestial feasting, only tough skin drying rapidly and stinking in the heat of the sun, and horns of antelopes, scales of anteaters, porcupine quills, tusks of boars, hairy tails and a few bones lay around the terrain. This was the chance Joha had been waiting for. He chose some of the larger pieces of hide, cut off remains of limbs, heads and tails and began to prepare them by scraping away hairs and the softer parts on the underside. It was a long and difficult task, the dry skin unwieldy. He had to bash, fold and roll it each day to retain some pliability until eventually presenting Moogi and Toma with bags gathered up in folds, through the ends of which he cut slits for threading pieces of thong as a drawstring. In this way he made carrier pouches for all of them. The longer they dried, the stiffer they became and only constant handling kept them usable.

Although Joha knew such essential things had to be made for their journey, he was increasingly impatient with every day that passed. It made him uneasy to sit about whittling sticks and preparing skins when the direction finder within him drummed 'Go! Go! Go!' at every sunrise. His boredom was mitigated by watching Moogi working, sitting on the ground, her long hair falling in strands about her, rocks placed between her spread legs, her firm youthful breasts pointing upward as she raised an arm to hit one stone with another. His physical responses to her confused him. Was this a child or woman?

Her body and features were so different from the females he had known, making it impossible to judge her maturity. She had grown, though nothing like Toma who was up to his shoulder and filling out. All Joha had to go by was her body language and the eyes that shone at him, raising his excitement.

When she hugged him for bringing her a choice bit of fruit he felt his ora swelling, so much so that he had to walk away for fear she would notice. He urgently wanted to mate with her but the thought of how she or Toma might react stopped him.

Increasingly he wanted to hold her in his arms, as he had done when they came ashore from crossing the river after she saved them with the antelope carcass. He frequently sat as close as possible to her, held her hand and stroked it and waited for her eyes to tell him she liked his attention. At such times it was difficult not to take her behind bushes to do what he used to do with those willing females at his old camp.

When near her his worry about the enforced lull in their journey stopped and his usual inner voice was replaced by one telling him Moogi was not his child, and her breasts and buttocks looked like those of a female ready to be taken if only he knew how.

One night he felt a tug at his hand and waking found Moogi pulling his arm before crawling out of the shelter. It was surely a signal that something was up and he followed quietly, not to wake Toma. Outside, the crescent moon spread a little sheen over land and vegetation as she pulled him behind a bush and took hold of his ora. He had such a shock that he stood still for a moment but then the memory of past similar experiences with females shot through his mind, the meaning of her action dawned and all his passion for her concentrated. He pulled her down gently and entered her with some difficulty, Moogi helping by moving her body to receive him. At last he was able to copulate, and so suffused was Joha's mind with its drive that he was incapable of thought, and Moogi despite her relatively small size responded like a female leaving childhood behind. In between his exertions when he took a moment's rest from his frenzy, he wondered whether he was doing 'bad-bad' to his child but forgot about it next moment enticed by urge and pleasure.

When he ejaculated it was with a cry of pain, so sudden and fierce was the force of the expulsion. Then he came to, moved off Moogi and lay sweating and confused, not knowing how all this was happening. Moogi, released, turned to hug him, and reassured he took her between his arms and pressed his mouth several times on her face in response until all at once he realised how exposed they were. He sat up with a jerk, glanced fearfully round realising he had not a weapon on him, and pulling Moogi up led her quickly to the shelter.

They were not aware that Toma, hearing strange noises nearby, had awoken and finding the other two gone, had crept out to look for them. Their lovemaking drew him near. He took a long look but saw Joha and Moogi oblivious of all around them, closely linked and emitting grunts and low squeals of pleasure. He had never seen such interaction before and stood watching with growing interest. His father was exerting himself on top of Moogi who had her arms round him, and therefore this could not be a fight as he had first feared. Listening to Joha breathing as though running after prey, Toma concluded that whatever it was he was doing with Moogi must be hard work; in response Moogi was straining in rhythm and crying out with pleasure and not pain. The more he stared in the dim light, the more Toma could not understand what was going on. The fact that the other two were so absorbed in what they were doing, not even noticing his presence, made him uneasy. What about wild animals? At any moment some prowling flesh could pass by and take advantage. He retraced his steps silently to the shelter, fetched his weapons and sat, hunting stick in hand, to watch over the other two from a little distance. After a while the noise of their exertion stopped, presumably they had fallen asleep. All the more reason why he must keep watch.

That was how Joha and Moogi found him, sitting in front of the shelter nervously clutching the hunting sticks.

'You here?' Joha queried.

'I stop buhu,' said Toma in a voice implying it was surely right to do so. 'You finished?'

Joha grunted, Moogi said, 'Yes, we go sleep.'

They crawled through their shelter's opening and settled, Joha wondering whether he would have to send Toma away.

At dawn Joha woke with a feeling of satisfaction, increased when Moogi's eyes told him she wanted more of mating when he was ready. He realised his desperation to find a female was over, he did not need another now. Moogi had shown she was ready for his ora by making the first move like all those other females. His mind, clear after the relief of an ejaculation into a female instead of the previous unsatisfactory results achieved by rubbing his ora, accepted their mating was 'good-good' and more pleasure lay ahead.

There was however still that cause of unease, Toma. Had he been watching them? Was he going to try the same with Moogi? Toma and Moogi were always together, always talking, and making that 'ha-ha!' noise, and sometimes when the camp was near a river she went to sit in the water or threw it over herself, and then Toma often followed her. Were they mating when he was out of sight? He felt a rising anger. He would not tolerate Toma having Moogi, Moogi was his. Should he send Toma away as the big males had once chased him off? He glanced at his young ones. No, he could not do it, Toma was only up to his shoulder and not yet fully-grown. He would first watch to see what they were up to and then act if necessary.

Moogi's actions during the night decided him that she had recovered from her flood ordeal, so there was nothing to stop them from moving on. At last his inner voice could have its way. He faced the other two and said, 'We go,' with renewed assurance. The sun rose to warm the air, the slight mist disappeared from swampy patches. They picked up their sticks, handaxes, food bags with small gourds of water tied to them, the necks stuffed with grass, and followed him out of camp.

Later that day when out of Joha's earshot, Toma asked Moogi what she had been doing with his father outside the shelter. In her lively form of talk she told him about the 'good' of having a male's ora to touch or to have inside her.

'I do with you?' he asked hopefully.

'No, I Joha's female; another female for Toma.'

'I have no female,' he said sadly.

She promised to help him find one. Seeing Joha was looking in their direction they went up to him, Moogi putting her arms round his middle.

Toma explained so that his father would understand. 'Moogi your female; I look for other female. Moogi help me.'

Thus the matter was settled to Joha's relief and he would not have to abandon his son. His memory of almost losing him always remained. No, he would never send Toma away. Now as before they must look for a camp with females but for Toma this time.

Wordlessly he growled his agreement, getting a tight hug from Moogi and a grateful look from his son. Toma however, with Moogi as a source of information, did not want to let the subject of the male ora rest. For some time he had watched surreptitiously when his father rubbed his during unguarded moments. When his own started to swell and made him feel excited in a way he could not explain, he felt a desire to rub it and having seen Joha do so, he did the same and found some relief. Once more he waited until Joha was walking ahead and then asked Moogi about it. She was sure rubbing his ora was 'good'. It would be even better when they found him a female who could do it for him, or he might push his ora into her, in which case it would be 'good-good'.

The next evening when it came to making the shelter Joha told his son to build one for himself, and Toma worked out in his mind that his father did not want him to have to stay awake watching over him and Moogi doing the 'good-good' thing.

One day each trying to beat the other Moogi and Toma ran ahead, although the latter now always won, when Joha stopped to listen to a sound coming from far off. It was not part of the daily noises of the savannah or the forest, nor was it like the death scream of a baboon. He called to the other two urgently. When they hurried back he made them sit down to listen. At first there was stillness, silence, only broken by rustlings, the beating of a bird's wing or its squawk. Then after a while the strange noise reached them again. It was unmistakably males shouting.

Joha and Moogi exchanged glances of hope. Could this be strangers, fuzimo? Might they meet with a group who would have a female for Toma? Joha presumed a hunt was taking place and when the shouts drew nearer he looked towards a distant clump of trees expecting the hunters to appear from their dark shadows. Instead silence resumed. The three began walking swiftly in the direction of the noise fearful that the hunt was over and they would lose contact with the hunters. Toma offered to run ahead to find them but Joha remembering previous experience put a staying hand on him.

As they stood uncertain what to do there came the sound of running feet and a male tore past, almost throwing himself forward. Behind him followed two others in equal hurry wielding sticks and cudgels. Joha gave a warning growl and the three threw themselves to the ground in the grass and lay as still as stones.

The strangers caught up with the single runner, pushed him to the ground, belabouring him with their cudgels as he lay screaming. He flung up his arms to ward off their blows but the beating persisted with renewed vigour until he lay still, blood running from head, body and limb. Meanwhile a larger group of males shouting angrily and brandishing their weapons emerged from the surrounding scrub. On reaching the spot they stuck their hunting sticks into the body with satisfied howls before withdrawing them bloodied. The murderers picked up their victim's belongings, and while the three cowered in the grass terrified of discovery, the whole lot went off in the direction of the trees, still shouting.

Joha kept a warning hand on the other two, afraid that stragglers or possibly the family of the hunted male might arrive any moment. But all that appeared was a flock of vultures that began to pick and tear at the body, fighting one another in their usual manner. Toma wanted to go and see whether the male was dead but Joha restrained him knowing what would happen next. Within moments two lions came strolling up to the corpse followed by a pack of hyenas alerted by seeing circling birds in the sky, and beast and birds snarled and squawked as they picked the flesh and cracked the bones.

This was a new danger but seeing the animals were fully occupied the three dared to crouch and run to cover until the terrain emptied and they went on their way in silence after the ghastly scene they had witnessed. Toma walked in front, his body language expressing disappointment and perhaps despair, and behind him Joha and Moogi exchanged a few words of regret that they could not find any friendly fuzimo.

That night for a while Joha made himself camp-guard by walking round it, peering nervously in the dark uncertain of every bush and shadow. Where were those strangers living, nearby? Could there be one of them lurking behind a tree or lying flat on the ground ready to jump at him? After a long vigil he woke Toma and told him to take over because his eyes could no longer distinguish one shape from another.

At dawn the three picked up their belongings and hurried away as fast as they could, Joha leading unfalteringly since his inner voice always indicated the direction of the safari.

After this failed encounter with a fuzimo group Moogi sensed that Toma was increasingly unhappy, because he no longer challenged her to race him, sat apart at resting places and ate sparingly. Joha noticed nothing, always too absorbed in finding small buhu to kill for their food and intent on searching the horizon for any sign of green vegetation indicating a waterhole or river. He was also vigilant about strangers, fearing an encounter might result in a threat rather than a welcome.

At night now that his sex urge found outlet he could hardly wait to take his female, and often when the shelter proved too confining, the two went outside a little distance from Toma's and made love. The latter had long learned to discern the slightest movement, waking when his ears picked up their creeping tread. Apart from genuinely wanting to guard them from danger he was still very curious about what they were doing, especially after Moogi's explanations, and being as adept as his father in creeping up on buhu, he moved as near as he dared to see him pushing into Moogi who made strange noises which must surely be the result of that 'good-good.'

As he watched time and again, excited by their passion and climax, he became increasingly envious and resolved to make his own feelings known.

It had been a long march with little rest even in the greatest heat of the day, and they had seen no sign of water when Joha called a halt allowing them to sit down in silence, grateful to rest before starting on shelter building.

After a while Toma announced abruptly, 'I want female.'

It took Moogi a moment to realise what he was saying before replying, 'Those fuzimo bad. No female from bad fuzimo.'

'I want Moogi.'

Joha growled something unintelligible and Moogi repeated in the spirit of previous words, 'Moogi for Joha, other female for Toma.'

'My ora sore, it want Moogi,' Toma persisted. 'Joha put ora in Moogi, me want same.'

Moogi got up leaving his father to sort out the problem and wandered some way off to start breaking twigs for the shelter. She felt sad about Toma: he was growing big and surely needed a female badly.

There was a sizable bundle of branches waiting to be carried back when there was a howl and shriek that brought her up short. Toma was crying out for help and Moogi took off towards the spot where, now that she was able to see what was going on, father and son seemed to be fighting. Joha had his big hands round the neck of his son and was forcing him to the ground. Moogi stopped in front of them, taking the situation in.

'Stop!' she commanded, breathless from her fast sprint. 'Stop!'

Joha loosened his grip, looked at Moogi and without a word walked off. Toma straightened up spluttering to regain his breath, his hands feeling his throat, and tears running down his cheeks.

'Sit,' Moogi said, seeing he was trembling and looked as though he was going to fall over, and began massaging his neck and stroking the hair on his head to calm him.

Joha walked away not caring where he was going. After an initial few angry words his fury had spilled over. A young male threatened to take his place, his female, his right to her. Still worked up he stumbled over a root. That Toma, that young male not yet fully grown wanted Moogi, wanted his ora to enter her. Joha clenched his fists and growled, increasing his pace in agitation not knowing what he should do and not aware that he was storming along in a wide circle.

After a while calmed somewhat, his mood went into reverse; he thought of how he had wanted to kill Toma, kill his child. Now remorse hit him, and hard.

'Toma, Toma,' he kept murmuring to himself, realising how much his son meant to him and unable to understand what he had tried to do. Memories of a little male child running everywhere and eating everything small enough to fit his mouth; the child in danger from those strange females; Toma playing with Moogi; their chases and mock fights; his first kill of an antelope; Toma asking for a female, all went through his mind. Why had he tried to kill him? He put his hands over his ears to shut out Toma's voice in each scene and stumbled on, regardless of thorny branches.

Finally weary from so many conflicting emotions in such a short space of time, he threw himself down, burying his face in his hands, his mind exhausted.

He was almost asleep when he heard something moving and automatically reached for the weapons he suddenly realised were not to hand. It was the short period between twilight and dark; keeping perfectly still was the safest thing to do.

'Joha?' said a voice followed by a deeper one. 'Joha?'

It was Moogi and Toma, both had followed his trail of broken twigs and trodden grass the best they could in the fading light.

He stood up relieved as they came pushing branches aside to reach him, Moogi moving forward first and hugging him.

Nobody said anything on the way back to the campsite, and after building two flimsy shelters in the failing light, Moogi and Joha bedded down for the night in the larger, leaving Toma to sleep in his smaller one.

BAD AND GOOD

The Lady Archaeologist was busy. Very busy, Baratu concluded, from the fact that she had not flown in for a while. The explanation came when he received an invitation to attend a meeting at the Museum lecture hall. Palaeoanthropologists interested in African fossils would be gathering to read papers on latest finds and research. Over the radiophone he asked her whether the invitation had been sent him by mistake.

'I'm not a scientist,' he remonstrated.

'You are asked to attend because many of my colleagues would like to meet you.'

'But they will ask me questions I can't answer.'

'Then just say so,' she replied emphatically. 'You are to take the next returning supply flight. I've already phoned your wife that you're coming.'

So it was that Baratu found himself in the front row of the Museum hall when the Lady Archaeologist introduced the subject.

'Hello everyone, hope you have all had a rest after your various flights. I'll start with a few remarks, after which we will have coffee followed by the first lecture.

'On the tables, you see assembled some replicas of representative fossils marking our human history in Africa. Of course we must add that new finds will inevitably take us a step further. Where we couldn't get a model we have left a name card, so that nobody can complain that their favourite fossil is forgotten. Many thanks to those who contributed so generously.

'Discovery shows evolution trying out variation from early semi-bipedal primates through to Homo erectus and early Homo sapiens. Personally I often wonder whether these different branches, some of which lived contemporaneously, ever made friends, or did they fight each other should they have met in those long ago forests and plains of East Africa.

'All these surmises apart, I'm sure the one thought that crosses all our minds is, can we with our larger brains interpret our many finds and come to some sort of conclusion about the interaction of our ancestors. Are fossils of differing hominin branches ever found together or even near each other? And precisely that will be the subject of our first talk.'

The scientists clapped their approval and straightaway launched into a hubbub of discussion before the promised coffee and lecture.

– – – – – –

In the part of the continent where the three travellers continued their journey for very many dawns and nights, and where the deluge of rain had caused so much flooding followed by the blooming of the savannah, the reverse had set in resulting in a vicious drought. Grazers stripped leaves from bushes and trees making them look skeletal and cropped grass to its roots until the ground showed through, yellow or brown. Animals in turn suffered the same fate by dying of dehydration or being eaten by others. This abundance of flesh also meant that Joha, Moogi and Toma did not need to make a detour every time they saw predators but walked past them without arousing interest. They were therefore able to cover greater distances, although Joha's inner voice still urged speed.

One day on their journey ever onward without a day's rest, Moogi stopped in her tracks, held her tummy with both hands and gave a cry of alarm. The males stopped to see what was wrong.

'It go,' she said with a perplexed face.

The other two looked at her front with interest.

'It go?' queried Toma but Joha without hesitation replacing her hands with one of his large ones declared, 'Child here.'

As he withdrew his hand, they could see her tummy moving of its own accord, humping slightly to one side and then rounding out.

She stood dumbstruck, looking down on what she had not noticed up to then, her distended middle. 'Child here?' she echoed incredulously and felt herself to see where it was.

Toma equally astonished felt over her tummy but withdrew his hands hastily when his fingers were pushed up ever so slightly by something moving under them. He looked at his father for an explanation, getting the same answer: 'Child here.'

Joha having seen it all before put a reassuring arm round Moogi as his memory flashed back to the alarming and yet fascinating birth of his sons.

He decided to call for more rest stops. Toma would carry Moogi's food bag and they would give her all the titbits foraged as they went. If there was a child in Moogi, it also needed feeding. The thought of it made him feel excited and heightened his passion for her. On their own now in the nightly shelter he asked for her sexual favour by placing his ora in her willing hands, and as his pleasure mounted he fondled and stroked her, aware that he could no longer lie on top of the distended tummy that he had previously assumed to be a sign of eating so much flesh.

Days later the flat savannah gave way to hills barring their way. Joha's inner voice told him to go round but the thought of standing on top looking at a possible route beyond as he had done before from smaller rises, tempted him to climb up via a shoulder of the escarpment. Moogi brought up the rear slow in gait, and Toma stayed with her until they reached the top just before sunset when the slanting rays lit up a steep slope on the other side. Grateful for rest she sank down, while the other two passed round the food bags containing spongy tubers to slake their thirst and satisfy their hunger. The males began building shelters while she sat and watched, though once she would have been the first to pull up tufts of grass for bedding.

At dawn next day a mist in the valley below decided Joha to wait until the view cleared. Toma, sitting on a rock, peered down the slope for a possible descent leading to a snaking line of vegetation that promised a watercourse. After a while he shouted, 'Fuzimo!' as he pointed excitedly at some moving dots. 'That fuzimo there, walk, stop. There, there.'

The other two argued, 'Not fuzimo, buhu.'

'Buhu with many legs. That fuzimo… ' and he held up two fingers.

All three began pointing and arguing about the moving dots that in their eyes had either two legs and two arms, or four legs.

Finally Joha suggested, 'We go, see, come back …' and he indicated where in the sky the sun would be on their return. 'Moogi stay.'

There were no animals to be seen on their hill, and anyway with the predators satiated, the alleged fuzimo in a camp below, Moogi would be safe. She agreed readily, realising Joha had in mind the importance of making contact with a stranger group but on peaceful terms for the sake of finding Toma a female.

'Go, look. Fuzimo good - fuzimo bad,' she reminded them as they left.

The sun made its steady progress across the sky, its hot rays beating down until the ground was burning under Moogi's feet. The others would take long to return, she must prepare for the wait with defensive weapons to hand. No moment was ever quite safe. She broke off some of the dry thorn bush and dragged the branches to surround the gwa.

Hand-size stones lay all around asking to be placed in a heap inside the enclosure together with her hunting sticks, cudgel, food pouch with handaxe and a gourd water carrier. Lastly she gathered some twigs with leaves that looked edible even if going dry.

When she rested after the activity her tummy gave a small lurch. She clutched it with an exclamation of 'Eh!' and examined herself, not difficult since her tummy was resting on her thighs as she sat. There was something in there for sure, Joha was right. A child? How would it come out? Being in there - she stroked her tummy - it must come out through her mouth. The thing must be tiny, and she chewed on the drying leaves, put a finger in her mouth and felt the cavity for size. A tiny male she imagined; it would pop out and start walking round her. But child zebras and buffalos, antelopes, giraffes and elephants, all came out from the back of the females. Once out, they stood up on longish legs and walked with the herd. There? she wondered, and felt her bottom. Her fingers came to a hole that she recognised. This was where her turds plopped out and the child would be small like turds. Choosing some of the pebbles she tried piling them up in the dust in the shape of a tiny Toma but it only looked like a heap of stones.

That thing within her moved again first to one side, then the other, a pleasant ticklish sort of feeling that made her laugh. She must ask Joha how she could push it out like her turds. He and Toma were taking long. The sun had moved right over her head and though now and then she peered at the land below, there was no further sign of fuzimo. She rose, stretched and noticed the welcome emptiness about her except for insects and birds gliding over the slope. They must walk on the warm breeze she could feel but where were their feet? She decided to imitate the birds but wondered where to tuck away her legs. Stepping high as if to mount a rock she did not get airborne and tried again, this time spreading her arms out with hands flapping up and down the way the vultures and hawks moved their wing tips but she still did not rise. Perhaps the thing when it came out, so small, might do it.

Thirsty now, she looked around in vain to find tubers as they had finished their supply. The water gourd was almost empty. In the distance not far from the fuzimo they had seen was a green patch where perhaps Joha and Toma could fill their water carriers. Something else came into her mind: when she drank the water must satisfy the thing inside her, and when she ate, food must go into its mouth. Moogi was fascinated, longing for the day it would come out, and she began addressing it in her lively manner.

'Toma and Joha go there.' She stood up and pointed. 'You see? They bring water, come back soon,' and she imitated Joha's arm movement to indicate where the sun would be. 'You want food?' she asked, looking down at her tummy. 'I eat,' and she hastily chewed the last of her supply.

Meanwhile the sun was running down to the horizon and past the point Joha had indicated.

'Eh!' The child had moved again. 'You want to see?' asked Moogi of her tummy. 'Look,' and she pushed her abdomen with her hands in the direction the males had descended the hill. Listening for them she grew tired, sat down inside the enclosure she had made and catnapped.

Nothing stirred. The shadows lengthened, a cool waft of air brushed her skin, the forerunner of dusk and nightfall. To shake off the strain of waiting and its boredom that the child might be experiencing as well, she said soothingly, 'Joha and Toma come soon,' and then sang the words quietly in a lilting tune.

She found her throat somewhat dry and had a sip from the water carrier, careful to leave just enough for the males in case they had found no water.

'You want some?' she addressed the child again and took another sip on its behalf.

When the slope she had been watching disappeared into an engulfing dark that sheen from the stars could not penetrate, she gathered her weapons, crept into her shelter and sat listening intently for the voices she hoped to hear. Night noises took over from the quiet day, rustling and snuffling, night birds called and bats twittered. Far away a hyena shrieked its laugh, a lion bawled, a small creature nearby piped a terror-stricken squeak, all familiar sounds Moogi hardly heard as she strained to catch Joha's grunt or Toma's call. Sometime during the night it came, a quiet 'Moogi!' though she had not heard a twig break. She answered, then told her tummy, 'They come, you get more water.'

Exhausted, the males sank down outside the shelter and handed her a full gourd.

'Fuzimo?' she enquired. They did not answer. 'Female?'

The two males remained tongue-tied except for Joha's, 'We go!' as though it were dawn.

'We go?' Moogi echoed, astonished.

'We go!' Joha's voice was a command, and slinging her food pouch and gourd over his shoulder with his own, he told her to follow Toma, while he brought up the rear close behind. They moved stealthily between boulders and bushes down the hill in the bright African night. At the bottom when Moogi thought they would stop, Joha motioned her on in silence. He was so big and powerful-looking and so obviously determined, that neither of the other two would have thought of remonstrating.

Something was wrong, Moogi realised but it was not the moment to press for answers. Joha urged them on relentlessly, Toma led in silence and she put one foot before the other and kept up the best she could. Occasionally they stopped as if by the males' common consent, though never for long.

Zebra were clearly visible under the stars but darker buhu loomed up all of a sudden or were avoided because Toma heard their munching and tummy rumblings. By dawn Moogi too weary to speak up, sank down and went to sleep on the spot. When she woke, Joha and Toma were sitting near her as though they had not moved.

Feeling refreshed, Moogi could not suppress her curiosity any longer. 'Say about fuzimo,' she insisted.

Toma looked at his father. 'We say?' he enquired.

Joha grunted his assent.

Haltingly at first Toma began relating the previous day's events. On their way to find the fuzimo, Joha had told him his plan that if the strangers were friendly they would ask for a female but if they looked fierce they would try to abduct one. Toma was worried about this possibility until his father told him how he had taken his mother from the old camp during the days when he had been lonely.

'Joha say he see female in grass, she frightened, want to shout, he put hand on mouth, take her on shoulder, he run.'

'She stay with me,' Joha added triumphantly. 'She make Toma.'

Moogi had never thought of Toma having a mother. Her own was long forgotten.

Toma went on to tell her that they had found the fuzimo camp hidden in a thicket. Joha had whispered to him that they were to take a stealthy look to find out whether they seemed friendly. While they were peering through branches they became aware of another person about to squat down quite nearby. It was a woman because they could see her breasts.

Joha signalled that they should carry out their plan. Toma crept up on the female and jumped on her, at the same time clamping a hand over her mouth while his father pinned her arms down when she fought back kicking and scratching.

'We see big head, big teeth like baboon,' Toma explained. 'No want that female. We run.'

They left her screaming and ran for their lives. Hearing shouts behind them they shinned up a tree and from a distance saw the fuzimo surrounding the female and pulling her down. They tied her hands back and her feet together with thongs. The two up the tree thought they would drag her back into camp but instead one of them began pulling her in the opposite direction along the ground to her dismal wails and cries. The other fuzimo followed, adding to the noise with a lot of shouting.

The female was not like the fuzimo in camp, Joha explained in his halting way. She was a stranger.

'She look for male,' added Toma.

They watched as she was hauled over sticks and stones screaming, one man taking over from another. They dragged her round and round until her body went limp and silent and she was left in the thicket.

Toma put his head in his hands at the memory and Joha patted him sympathetically on the shoulder. They had been too worried to climb down from their tree, fearing that they as strangers would suffer the same fate. They waited for sunset before daring to descend from their hideout to creep away back to Moogi.

'Bad-bad fuzimo,' she said quietly. She now understood their reticence in talking about what they had seen. How glad she was her males had got away from such a terrible situation.

Patting her tummy gently, Moogi informed the child of what was going on. 'Toma want female, female like baboon, Toma no want baboon, bad-bad fuzimo kill her,' and turning to him she said consolingly, 'we look for good female.'

In the returning sunlight she saw his sad face and despondent look and silently agreed that it seemed almost an impossibility.

As they journeyed on, Joha greeted every dawn with the shout, 'We go!' Toma bleary eyed lurched into action; Moogi clutched her enlarged tummy and stumbled forward determined not to be left behind.

Finding enough water was their constant worry. It had disappeared from riverbeds and only determined digging brought the reward of a trickle to fill their gourds. Wildlife had moved away, perhaps in the knowledge of where a drink could be found. Despite urging by the other two that they should follow the animals, Joha refused.

Nightmares of deep waters on which he floated inside a shelter about to capsize terrorised his nights so that he woke sweating. Moogi sensing trouble woke to find him sitting up, arms desperately grasping at air.

The fuzimo and their dreadful deed were not mentioned again. The males were occupied foraging as they went along and Moogi concentrated on keeping up with them under a white-hot sky. It was therefore exciting when they came across a grass-lined shallow hole sheltering warthog piglets that promised a succulent meal. Before one could be caught there was a rush and roar and a sow came charging at them from a patch of tall plants. The three scattered, Moogi stepped up onto a low branch of the nearest tree, the males jumped out of the way while raising their hunting sticks for the kill.

The hefty sow stopped in its tracks with a snort, stiffened its legs, made an about-turn and came running at Joha's legs with its head of tusks lowered for attack. The males threw their sticks but only struck the ground where the animal had been a moment before. Moogi from the safety of the tree shouted to them to join her but Joha jumped aside and raised his second stick to attack, at which moment the sow made another strategic turn about and rushed at Toma who was retrieving their weapons. Once again Joha's missile hit the ground instead of the animal. Seeing Toma attacked, Joha picked up his stick and ran to help him, Moogi shouting frantically to both to get up on her tree. So fast was the sow's attack that Toma only just avoided being gored, and now both males lost all caution and thoroughly rattled made repeated attempts to get the animal with their throwing sticks. The scene went wild with Moogi shouting, the sow rushing from one target to the next, and sticks flying through the air in all directions. Finally the piglets streamed from their nest hollow and ran about squealing with fright, ignored by their mother as well as the irate males, until the sow realising the danger to her family suddenly stopped the skirmish, gave some warning snorts and trotted away, her piglets following behind tail in the air. Joha and Toma were so surprised by the sudden ceasing of battle that they stood breathless and staring stupidly after the departing family.

Exhausted from shouting instructions to which nobody had paid any heed, Moogi descended from the tree uncertain as to whether she should be angry or laugh. The valuable opportunity of a good meal had been missed. Disgruntled they picked up all their belongings dropped during the mêlée, Joha turned in the direction they had been walking and they marched on, Moogi having to take a few running steps now and then to keep up. Joha was reminded of how small she had been when he rescued her and she had jogged to keep up with them. A glance at her bobbing breasts and wobbling protruding tummy made him feel proud he now had an adult female. A surge of desire went through him as he realised how 'good' she was, not like the strange one they had so nearly captured by mistake.

He took her hand and helped her along. That child in her tummy, when would it come out? He stopped Moogi in her tracks, put his hands on her middle and felt for its movement.

'Child want out,' he said earnestly to her.

Moogi liked feeling his big hands so gently placed on her but she had no answer to his statement.

Child however was some time coming and meanwhile Moogi had to keep up her marching the best she could.

A mountain now loomed on their horizon, taller than anything they had seen before and growing in size with each day they drew nearer until trees could be seen on its slope. Moogi let out a whoop when they discovered a riverbed with wet sand. Walking along the middle of the course they reached water, which further down had become dissipated in the hot ground of the savannah. The land sloped up gently, covered by scrub vegetation with green leaves giving way to occasional trees and ever greener undergrowth. The clear water in the stream increased in volume, splashing over rounded rocks and pebbles glinting in the sun.

Before them stretched a meadow of grass so lush and soft that they trod carefully and bent to feel the blades between their fingers. Beyond, the mountain slope was covered with forest almost to the summit where it gave way to a barren-looking rim.

The sun's heat was mild, insects hummed, elephants and rhino grazed in the distance on the edge of the trees, seemingly unaware of the intruders.

The three stared at the scene in wonder and then at each other, the same question in their eyes. How could there be such a place when the land they had just traversed was devastated by drought? Moogi sat in the stream sloshing water over herself while Joha and Toma gathered leaves, flowers and fruit for a meal. They had seen nothing like this for a long time let alone ever and became intent on pleasurable foraging, each in a different direction. When they returned to give Moogi food, she was not to be seen. As there were no predators around and not likely to be, elephants and rhino being too big for them to kill, and no sign of strangers, father and son sat by the river unperturbed by her absence and ate, expecting her to come into sight soon. When she did not turn up they called her name ringing across the meadow and receiving no answer began to search, walking downhill in the direction from which they had come.

The landscape was so peaceful that it was difficult to think of anything happening to her, and without footprints to follow it was evident that she had walked in the stream.

Joha searched the terrain along one bank, Toma the other. They had foraged long for the meal, they realised, and during that time Moogi could have walked quite a way, even at her slowed pace. The sun was some way from the horizon, no worry about nightfall and so father and son wandered at leisure, unable to avoid the temptation of picking choice edibles in between their calls.

When Toma signalled he was hearing something, both stopped to listen, moving their heads this way and that in the best direction to catch any noise. Above the gurgling of the water came a sound only Moogi could make. They hurried round the next bend and there she was, sitting in the stream with her back to them. She was singing, and coming nearer they saw she was holding the newborn child on her knees, absorbed in looking at it dripping with water, washed and shiny.

Joha squatted beside her until she put it in his big outstretched hands. 'Amu,' she told him.

'Amu,' said Joha in a hushed voice, cradling the child and looking at it with an ecstatic expression. 'Child, for me.'

Toma who had watched with bewilderment put a finger out to touch the child's tiny wrinkled hand, which immediately clasped it tightly. Joha gently loosened the grasp and marched off back to camp, holding Amu in the crook of his arm, a shielding hand over her head.

'We have food,' Toma said lamely. 'You come?'

Moogi tried to rise but with difficulty. In the water near her, tiny fish were gathering round something like a big liver and a length of what looked like gut. Toma helped her up and she managed to walk back to where Joha was still cradling Amu in his hands.

Moogi was ravenous, pleased with all the other two had left her to eat and asking for more. Amu slept and Toma went off to refill the food bags.

After the shelters had been constructed and Moogi sat holding her daughter with Joha close by, they passed the bags round to eat again and were absorbed in admiration of the newly born. Toma kept feeling the tiny feet, the spider-like fingers, and gently stroked the shock of hair so like Joha's on her tiny head.

Joha remarked on the difference between their previous camps and this one, the flowing water, green grass and abundance of hares. However, their attention inevitably returned to Amu amidst exclamations of 'Good-good!'

That night with Joha and Moogi in each other's arms in the shelter, Amu in a nest of dry grass, they were parents rather than lovers, too happy to speak, too satisfied to arouse each other.

At dawn Joha awoke with his inner voice urging him to get going. But he thought of the lush vegetation, the gurgling clean water, the new child, and saw no reason to leave just yet. The voice continued, urging departure. Joha turned a deaf ear.

Moogi emerged stretching her limbs and tried some tentative running steps, her load shed and her spirits high. A shrill cry from the shelter stopped her in her tracks.

'Food,' she said to herself, feeling as hungry as Amu must be and she fetched her out. Choosing the smallest leaves from a food pouch she was about to stick them in the child's open mouth when Joha stopped her, put a hand on her breast and squeezed her shiny nipple until a drop appeared.

'Food,' he told her.

'Food?' she queried, looking down at her breasts and then at the screaming Amu, unable to make the connection.

Joha lifted Amu's head until her open mouth was round the nipple. She opened her eyes, looked at her mother, clamped her mouth over it and began suckling. Moogi looked at the males and let out a peel of laughter.

'You good,' she told Joha who, satisfied with the whole turn of events, decided he would definitely postpone leaving for a few more dawns.

'GO!'

On their flight back to the fossil camp, the Lady Archaeologist and Baratu were surrounded by provisions: sacks of maize and bread flour, rice and beans, sugar, tins of meat, vegetables and fruit, containers of still water, a large thermos of ice cream for a treat, instrument components and implement replacements, batteries, laundry bags, the men's personal requirements among which was a basket of dried fish for the man from the shores of Lake Victoria.

The Lady Archaeologist put her book down, and staring through the window said, 'Good view of the Rift Valley today.'

'Why did those geologists always talk about it and volcanoes?' Baratu asked.

'Sit here beside me so I don't have to raise my voice over the engine noise and I'll explain. Oops! that's the updraught from the dry valley bottom,' she exclaimed when the plane gave a lurch just as Baratu moved into the seat beside her.

'You know about this rift in the earth's surface running 3,700 miles from Mozambique in the south of Africa to the Jordan Valley and crossing the great dome of upland Kenya. The rift divides into two, the eastern section has some small lakes and our prominent mountains on its rim, Kenya, Kilimanjaro and Meru, not to forget Ol Doinyo Lengai, which is still active, and Ngorongoro that blew its summit off long ago. In the western section, the rift played its part in forming the land surfaces for water to accumulate into lakes such as Malawi, Tanzania, Kivu, and Turkana. For us fossil hunters, the lakes prove most important because from earliest times they were a source of water for animals as well as hominins.'

Baratu listened attentively. 'But we also find hominins near volcanoes. What about the Laetoli footprints that Mary Leakey found?'

'Yes, the ash in which they were imprinted had come from the volcano Sadiman some forty miles away. The hominins were not necessarily living there but happened to be walking in the ash just before it rained and set their footprints solid for Mary to find.'

'Were there more eruptions before now? We don't hear of them these days,' Baratu asked. 'Perhaps we should look for fossils in places where there are ash deposits from these old mountains.'

'Possibly,' said the Lady absentmindedly and turned back to the view.

There we go, thought Baratu. Nothing is ever certain except that we all evolved from an ape tribe.

_ _ _ _ _ _

On the third dawn after Amu's birth, Joha awoke hearing a shout. 'Go!' It was his inner voice. He understood why it sounded angry, obviously because of his decision to delay departure. Yes, it was surely time to move, but when he crawled from the gwa to see the rising sun sparkling on the eddies of the stream, and squatted on the bank cupping his hands and drinking the ice-cold water, then smacking his lips, his answer to the voice was, 'Another dawn.' To show his defiance he plucked a handful of the green grass and chewing it to a soft pulp, spat the wad out with an exaggerated force.

Later when the sun was warm, Moogi sat in the river with Amu, splashing her and the males when they playfully tried a mock attack. She attempted running races with Toma whom she could no longer beat but still surpassed him at their game of hitting an agreed target with stones. Hers ricocheted with a clear 'ping'.

Meanwhile Joha had caught a hare and cut it up with the handaxe for a meal. Moogi wanted Amu to have some and it took a lot of persuasion by Joha to convince her that only the water from her breast was good for the child. Toma's mother had fed him on that and nothing else until he had some teeth, he told her.

Throughout the day while he and Toma continued to chase small buhu for butchering in preparation for their next journey, the inner voice persisted. 'Go, go now!' Wait for dawn, he kept replying in his mind. On his return to the camp for a rest he took Amu in his hands - so small and helpless. He flexed his muscles to make himself feel his superior size and experienced a flush of parental love streaming through his hands to the sleeping child, who opened her eyes wide and scrutinised him with such a knowing look that he was taken aback.

'Amu, you, child for me,' he told her. She shut her eyes again as if satisfied with the statement as he hugged her gently, the surge of his feelings bringing tears to his eyes.

That night distant screams and trumpeting from the forest awoke them. Joha quickly crawled out of the shelter, followed by Moogi carrying Amu, while Toma came running from his. They turned towards the bulk of the mountain silhouetted against the starred sky to hear a faint rumbling growing louder and louder as they stood frozen with uncertainty about what it could be and where exactly it was coming from. It passed under their feet like a roll of thunder lodged in the ground instead of reverberating round the sky, and receded.

Alarmed, especially as the animals were still screaming from the forest, Joha shouted, 'We go!'

Moogi and Toma had clung to each other in terror when the noise began and were still standing motionless when Joha shouted again and with greater urgency, 'We go!' and began trotting downstream. His voice was drowned in his ears by his inner one with the same message. He led the way alongside the water glinting under starlight, followed by the other two with Amu. Once more the growling, rumbling sound approached and with it the ground began to shake, so that they stumbled and held hands in support of each other before the noise faded and the earth was still.

Behind them there was an ear-shattering roar, the sky bloomed red, gushes of what seemed to be blood rose into the sky from the mountaintop with continuous claps of thunder. The noise went on, the earth trembled, the precious stream ceased flowing and a dust rained on their heads.

On and on they ran, stumbling, coughing, spluttering, eyes streaming. Joha forged through the undergrowth and between trees, finding his way in the night lit up by a red glow. Without glancing back he knew that if the ground sloped away they were moving in the direction of the thorn bush and the flat plain from which they had come. Away from the menace of the mountain. He took Amu into the crook of his arm and held the other hand protectively over her face. Despite repeated earth tremors he did not allow the others to stop, and fighting for breath they changed to running the easier way on the pebbles of the drying river. Toma dragged Moogi by the hand when she could run no longer, finally changing to taking Amu so that Joha could carry his female until she regained strength and breath.

Their flight ended at dawn when everything became quiet, even the repeated trembling of the ground. Joha, whose pace had slowed to a walk, stopped to let Moogi feed Amu, while he and Toma lay collapsed from their exertions. In the morning light the mountain looked as grey as the overcast sky.

'We go,' said Joha shortly, having arranged that they should take it in turns to carry Amu who had slept through everything and had only had one coughing fit.

Talking among themselves after the eruption, the travellers thought the mountain harboured some sort of sleeping creature disturbed by another animal on the side they could not see. It must have been fighting to its death, how else could they explain the blood they had seen spurting into the sky? Assuring each other the repeated thunder-like claps were the beasts' roars, they believed the fearful battle of such huge buhu had caused the rumbling and shaking of the ground, and the strange rain of dust that descended on them must have come from the beasts' hides. Animals who wallowed in mud and became caked with it and then fought one another, often set off showers of dust.

All day the three travellers walked in a wide circle to avoid going near the mountain, until coming into view of the reverse side they believed their surmises about fighting buhu were proved right. A cleaving gash starting halfway up the slope ran to the top where a misshapen craggy opening looked like a mouth grimacing in death. In the gullies they could see black matter that looked like congealed blood.

'Big buhu there,' Toma pointed at the summit.

'Other buhu eat arms, legs,' Moogi suggested.

'Dead!' Joha strained his eyes to make sure that what they saw as the remains of the animal were truly lifeless.

'See, buhu kill it, see.' Toma held Amu up and turned her to face the dead mountain.

For days afterwards they worried about where the victorious buhu had gone, a thing too awful to imagine. Their main concern, though, became the replacing of their belongings. Not only was the great buhu dead but also seemingly it had eaten all the trees and bushes round about, where there was a great plain of grass and little else. Moogi and Toma collected rocks to shape into handaxes and learned not to use black ones that fell to pieces. The lack of branches for whittling into throwing sticks made them particularly uneasy for it left them without weapons, and it was only after a few dawns and long marches that they saw their first groups of trees again.

An absence of food bags and gourds was another worry, though whatever the adults suffered in water shortage did not affect Amu who grew steadily on her mother's milk.

The terrible experience brought them closer in their relationships. Joha delighted in his daughter, rocking, tickling, and playing with her as often as they stopped. Moogi and Toma held hands wherever they went, reverting to their childhood habits when they had been inseparable. They hugged often, talked a great deal together, bathed whenever they reached a river, and when they went foraging disappeared from view to rejoin Joha unerringly further on along his trail.

Toma loved to carry Amu, showing her anything he thought interesting, and he understood better than her parents the warning grunts that preceded her emptying her bowels, so that he could hold her away from his body.

Joha was pleased with his son's attention to his daughter but most uneasy about his closeness with Moogi. He eyed the hugging with misgiving even though Moogi often came up to him, reached up to put her arms round his neck and stayed longer in his embrace. He had sex with her as often as he wished, waking up at dawn feeling so vigorous that he thought he could walk as far as the rising sun if his voice asked him.

Nevertheless he was unsure as to whether or not Moogi was allowing Toma sexual favours when they disappeared into the bush, returning triumphantly with dead lizards, rats, mice, tubers, an occasional tortoise or hedgehog all spiked on sticks, and birds' eggs carried carefully wrapped in leaves.

Toma, now fully grown, topped him and excelled in speed, hunting, whittling sticks and even knapping handaxes, and yet was still without a female. Joha feared he might carry out his wish of putting his ora in Moogi. He must watch him - must watch them or alternatively send his son away, but he also knew Moogi would not agree to such a move. Though he felt his son might take over from him, he assured himself that he was still their leader because his inner voice told him where to go, and he realised it had to be obeyed because in ignoring it they had almost been overcome by the dust from the fighting buhu.

He became more suspicious one day when the other two had jogged faster and disappeared beyond the next rise, whereas he had to slow his pace so as not to wake Amu asleep in the crook of his arm. It was easy to follow their trail in the sandy soil and presently he came upon them lying in the grass side by side. Joha's whole body gave a lurch of apprehension: this was it, he was certain they must have had sex. What should he do? His mind went blank with emotion he could not turn into coherent thought. Slowing his pace even more, trying to think of what to say, he came upon them from behind, blurting out, 'You taking his ora?'

Moogi, taking no notice of the question, patted the ground beside her and said, 'Lie.'

Joha in his complete confusion obeyed, and Amu waking up at that moment was placed on his chest.

Moogi pointed at the sky. 'Look!'

Joha did not know what there was to look at. Above them was the sun as usual and there were white things.

'Hoka,' she informed him, and sat up. 'Look, Amu!' and she rose, gave a few hops and flapped her arms up and down while thrusting her upper body forward in imitation of birds beating their wings.

Joha saw no birds in the sky and still looked perplexed.

'There,' Toma pointed at the clouds moving fast above them, and Moogi looked at Joha with laughing eyes, delighted at their discovery.

This could not be the result of taking Toma's ora, Joha concluded with relief. This was Moogi playing as in her childhood that seemed like the previous day. He acknowledged their fun and said, 'We go!' only to call a halt further on to tell them they must all walk together, no going ahead any more. There could be fuzimo anywhere. Had they forgotten their experiences? Joha always had the last word, and brought up to obey they walked together, carrying Amu in strict rotation thereby making better progress.

After leaving the slaughtered mountain and its empty countryside, there was a gradual increase of herds. Steaming dung indicated the presence of elephants. Those they had met grazing at the foot of the mountain had taken no notice of the travellers, who therefore had become unwary of the danger they might pose. Where in previous days Joha would have chosen to lead his family around or away from them, he now called a rest near a clump of trees where a herd with several young calves was tearing leaves from the branches.

Moogi carrying Amu went in search of the fat dung beetles so satisfying to eat. She put the child on the ground, and taking a twig, stirred in the pats to find the insects. One of the calves, as always inquisitive, came out of the undergrowth and frisked towards them. The huge bulk of the mother was not far behind. Seeing Moogi she obviously thought her calf threatened, her enormous ears flapped outward and she increased her pace.

Moogi, straightening up from picking a few beetles from a pat, wiping them with a leaf, ready to slip into her food pouch, became aware of the danger. She snatched her child from the ground and took off at a run.

At that moment the mother elephant gave a screech and charged. Joha and Toma shouted a warning. Too late, the elephant was almost upon her. The males rushed towards the cow shouting to distract her, threw their weapons but were too far to hit the animal, and were ignored as the cow focused all attention on Moogi and kept advancing at breakneck speed.

Instantly it became clear that Moogi burdened with Amu could not run fast enough to put her out of danger. The males picked up stones as missiles but the huge animal thundered on, intent on destruction. Hearing the heavy thud of the animal's feet right behind, Moogi suddenly stopped, turned, and with one free hand waving frantically above her, performed a wild up-and-down dance while screaming abusively at the hulk.

The elephant came to such a sudden halt that she skidded, recovered, peered at the thing in front of her, looked round for her calf and seeing it making off in fright into another thicket, trotted off to shepherd it back to the herd.

Moogi, handing the crying child to Toma, sank into Joha's arms while she caught her breath, her chest heaving. Meanwhile the cow and calf were back with the herd, grazing as though nothing had happened.

Joha could hardly bring himself to let go of his female. Still shocked from the realisation that the charging elephant was about to break every bone of what was Moogi and his child, he could not for the moment wipe the images from his mind. Toma was distracting Amu by walking up and down making soothing noises until she stopped crying. When everybody calmed down they continued their journey in silence, shaken by the experience.

It was after this event that Joha realised how important the female was in his life. He could not imagine Moogi dead and so he must look after her all the more.

She in turn realised how near she had come to death. What would have become of Amu if the elephant had reached them? She had once witnessed the frantic anger of a cow whose calf had strayed near a litter of warthogs. On that occasion the mother elephant had picked up one of the tiny creatures and smashed it to pulp on the ground.

Moogi told herself she must be careful for Amu's sake, especially since the child needed her 'water' of which she had so much that sometimes her breasts hung heavy and she had to support them with her hands while trotting.

The encounter with the elephant had made them careful once more not to walk near dangerous animals. The savannah they now traversed teemed with the usual herds of zebra, giraffe, antelopes, gazelles, rhino and buffalo, moving almost imperceptibly in a sea of tufted grass, while their attendant carnivores lolled on hillocks or in trees, watching the meals on legs drift by. This mass of animals caused the travellers a plague of ticks and fleas picked up from walking through the feeding grounds. At the end of each day after building their night shelters and while it was still light enough, each helped the other in removing these insects from their body-hair and limbs. Joha and Toma who had much more hair than Moogi suffered particularly, and occasionally they all had jiggers digging into their toes in the nail area, their soles being hardened almost to hide from constant walking. These insects had to be dug out with a sharp-tipped thorn, or else made the foot so itchy that it was impossible to sleep. Amu, who was beginning to crawl and made tentative movements to sit up, was the worst sufferer and as she screamed as soon as she realised it was her turn to be treated, one of the three had to hold her arms and feet before the jigger could be extracted.

As Amu grew quickly, much time was given by Mogi to teaching her daughter about everything they came across. 'Bad-bad' and 'good-good!' became Amu's first words.

Toma was always talking to her. 'This bad snake. You see! this, good buhu.' He played endlessly with her, running round in circles and stopping suddenly to make her laugh. She was still the little image of Joha, with a shock of short brown curls crowning the head in contrast to her mother's long black hair.

During the non-stop safari it was seasons that affected the family greatly. After the lusciousness of the volcanic region, and the walking larder of numerous herds, they experienced another dry season that threatened a drought, so that the three often had to dig to find water in dry riverbeds and depressions. Tubers had become equally scarce. Amu still suckled milk, though she had to be taught not to apply her erupting teeth to Moogi's nipples.

In time, the white clouds Moogi had called birds changed to grey, massed overhead and the rains came. Sunshine was blotted out by constant showers or rainstorms, and apart from the renewed supply of water and the awaking of dormant vegetation, the constant damp made their lives miserable. Each dawn the travellers crawled from their sodden shelters to an overcast sky and walked through another day of rain. The only one not miserable was Amu, who snuggled into Joha's hairy chest when the weather became fierce and just went to sleep.

Toma emerged with chattering teeth from his shelter each dawn until Moogi said, 'Toma sleep in our gwa.'

'Our gwa?' Joha exclaimed, thinking that was the last thing he wanted, but a glance at Moogi convinced him she would not have it otherwise. That evening their shelter was constructed wider than before, allowing Toma to creep in gratefully. Amu demanded to sleep next to him and Joha put her between himself and Toma, leaving Moogi to sleep on his other side. The rain pattered on the gwa's sodden covering all night, dripping increasingly on the sleepers. Rivulets of water swept through under the bedding of grass and leaves despite the runnels they had dug with sticks all the way round, but the heat of their bodies stopped the extreme cold Toma felt before.

Off again next day walking and jogging through constant rain, frogs were everywhere, almost too numerous not to be trodden on. At first they seemed such an easy food source until the three could not stomach them any longer.

Joha's inner direction finder urged him on when the others slowed down dejected. He was so used to the voice in his mind that he veered suddenly to take up another direction when ordered but couldn't explain it to the others.

They had walked into a rain-belt but in likewise manner one day they were out of it into sunshine and heat. The sun moved in a clear sky with few 'hoka', heat dried the muddy earth. Amu asked to be put down and crawled enthusiastically on warm ground. Moogi, not to be outdone by her daughter, flung down her new food pouch, let go of her hunting sticks and cudgel and ran round her, jumping over small bushes and rocks in exuberance.

The landscape around them bloomed again, leaf buds grew and unfurled, flowers buds developed, tubers increased in girth, and the air shimmered with rising damp. The four humans continued their journey with a will, plucking edibles as they walked or jogged between the greening bushes, Amu on her father's shoulders.

They had covered more than their usual walking distance and had stopped to rest in the hot afternoon sun when a strange light began to fill the land. At the same time a faint humming noise became audible. The three adults looked in the direction of the sound and saw a dark cloud obscuring the sun. They jumped up in alarm, staring at its fast approach. Joha glanced about him for a place to hide but they were in open country covered with grass and bushes as far as the eye could see. Before he could gather his wits the cloud was above them, a swarm of insects flying close together all going in one direction over their heads. The three adults ducked and huddled on the ground, holding on to each other in panic. Moogi snatched Amu to her breasts. There was nowhere to escape, the swarm filled all their visible sky and the flutter noise of uncountable wings droned in their ears.

When they dared to look up, a swirl of insects was breaking off from the main stream to land on every bush and blade of grass with a resounding thwack. Toma and Joha bent over double, hands over heads, Moogi held a hand over Amu in fear that the creatures would sting them but not one came anywhere near, though the chewing of leaves by these thousands of insects crackled everywhere around them.

After a while when the three dared to lift their heads again to peer at what was happening, the insects had eaten all the vegetation and were taking off to join the main swarm that had not stopped flying, leaving some stragglers behind that hopped about too satiated to leave the ground.

Moogi put out a hand to catch one, finding it looked like a big grasshopper. She pulled off its head, removed wings and legs and took a nibble. 'Good-good,' she said nodding at the others who, after watching her for a moment, tried the same. It was just as well that the insects were edible because some time later when the sky cleared and full sunlight returned, there was not a leaf or blade of grass to be seen. The savannah had been stripped bare. They could not even find the smallest bud on a bush for feeding Amu. Fortunately they had already weaned her to chewing cut up earth worms.

The adults, having filled themselves with the 'little flesh', were relieved that what had seemed an enemy they could not run from had turned out to be a source of food, even though this flesh had stopped their foraging for leaves. Amu drank from her mother's breast, then crawled among the remaining hoppers and had to be lifted away to prevent her from eating them, head, wings and legs.

After the feasting, Joha told his son to build his own shelter again and once more alone with his female that night celebrated with a long session of sex. Moogi had regained her slimness; she was joyful and less concerned with Amu's feeding, and her breasts no longer oozed milk but still looked full and shiny so that Joha desired her more than ever. With Toma out of the shelter, Joha's ora found relief once more in his making love slowly again and again, enjoying Moogi's uttered sounds of enjoyment, while Amu slept snug in a grass nest of dry bedding.

At dawn they crept out, facing a huge orange ball rising above a leafless vegetation where no shade would be found. Joha called to his son, 'We go,' but Toma did not emerge from his shelter. It was empty.

'Toma go?' he asked Moogi.

Moogi shouted, 'Toma! We go.' No answer came.

They scrutinised the ground and found single footprints in the sand, proving that he had not been abducted in the night nor been dragged out in his sleep by a predator.

Joha shouldered Amu for speed and they began to jog, following Toma's tracks that appeared again and again, clearly indicating the direction of his flight. However, no matter how much they hurried there was no catching up with him. With his size and stride he could outdistance them, even if they had all started out together.

Joha felt to blame. What had he done or said that his son should want to leave? Was he looking for something, a female?

Glancing at Moogi's troubled face he asked, 'He look for female?'

'Yes.'

'He say you?'

'No.'

There was no more to discuss, the matter was clear: Toma was not coming back. Joha handed Amu over and walked head hung in distress. Moogi followed equally saddened, and heart-heavy they continued on their way.

LOST

After the Lady Archaeologist and Baratu returned with the supply plane bringing the delicacies of ice-cream and dried fish, the fossil team responded with a renewed mood of enthusiasm for bone prospecting.

The geologists were back as well for a spell of working out the extent of the ancient lakebed.

Everybody was out early to walk the terrain before the heat forced a midday pause, and it was not long before one of the trial trenches fulfilled its promise and had to be enlarged when it yielded bones of extinct elephants and bovines.

Every evening at the long table in the work tent, fragments had to be sorted like a jigsaw puzzle, always in the hope that enough bones could be found to complete part or whole of an ancient animal's skeleton.

'No hippo this time,' remarked the Lady Archaeologist. 'Strange, since we know the finds come from the ancient lake shore.'

'Not necessarily,' said one of the geologists. 'We see that the shoreline receded or extended through time. Hippos came and hippos went.'

'And of course volcanoes were thrown up and the Rift Wall sank,' joked the Lady in the same vein.

'One big bang, look out, and we all sink down!' teased her colleague.

The fossil team looked at the scientists with worried faces. Were they making fun of scientific knowledge?

'Nature does everything gradually,' said Baratu soothingly. 'Surely the rifting happened bit by bit? One day an earthquake caused a section of ground to drop and then months or years later the next section collapsed and so on, forming the Rift Valley with steep sides.'

'I'm sure you're absolutely right,' agreed the Lady Archaeologist, changing to a serious tone. Then in a low voice as if talking to herself, 'Not only that but this rifting still continues and no one knows when the next phase may occur.'

– – – – – –

Despite many marches and a considerable passage of time, Toma's flight was still uppermost in the family's mind. Amu, who should have been too small to remember him, had his name repeated to her so often that she frequently asked for 'Oma'.

When she learnt to talk she called Joha 'Oha' and for a while her mother had to answer to 'Oogi'. After crawling, she attempted to rise only to collapse each time with peals of laughter. Giggling and laughing were her assets that sometimes moved Joha to lose his sad expression. He walked mostly head down, still searching for Toma's footprints, still hoping to find a sign of him somewhere some day. So intent was he that Moogi and Amu were often left behind and had to catch up to where he was waiting for them. In this way he had a rest but Moogi spent her days in non-stop walking, foraging, and sometimes carrying Amu, until she became even slimmer than her former self.

When they stopped to make camp, Amu, exhausted from using unsteady legs when her mother found her too heavy to carry and led her by the hand, sank down and immediately went to sleep, while her parents bedded her on soft grass and built their shelter round her.

Moogi remembered feeling equally tired when the child was still inside her. She could not forget Amu's birth: that walk along the river, the sudden sharp pain below her tummy, so severe that she had to sit, then another and another so agonising that she dragged herself to the riverbed thinking the water would soothe her. She was too far from the camp to shout for Joha or Toma and so afraid that a buhu would sense her weakness and attack.

But it had not happened. Amu came out where she least expected her to and though the pain was worse than passing hard turds, Moogi thought her good-good beyond anything she had ever seen.

'Amu!' Moogi looked at her child asleep. She was growing bigger and looked like a little Joha. Her mother stroked her face lovingly, remembering Toma often did the same.

Next day while pausing here and there to pick leaves and catch snails and worms she thought of him and wondered whether they would ever see him again. Tears came to her eyes, although she hoped he had found his female.

To get rid of such sad thoughts she told Amu, 'Make lo-lo,' and started singing, 'eeyaa, ehe-yaa, Amu, Amu, e-he-ya-ya.'

Amu tried to follow in her still rather toneless toddler's voice and the two walked on, Moogi improvising tunes and the child joining in.

A few dawns later the family started off together, though Joha soon became impatient with the slow progress and walked ahead. Moogi thought with sadness of how safe she had felt when Toma used to walk with her. He was always there to defend Amu from danger. What was the good of having Joha storming ahead? Gradually the distance between them increased, until a shout from him made her sling Amu on her back so that she could jog faster to catch up.

Joha, lost in his own thoughts, had been interpreting every spoor on the ground in addition to looking up and about him for possible danger until he saw something lodged in a distant tree that looked like a figure. His throat tightened with anticipation and he broke into a run. A dreadful sight met his eyes: not Toma fortunately but a fuzimo youth had been impaled in the tree. Eyes glazed in death stared from a distorted face; limbs hung listless over branches. The head was cleft and bloody but there were no marks of an animal's teeth or bird's beak on him. Joha was relieved and yet fearful. What fight had taken place here, was it Toma's work? He looked for footprints. None was visible and therefore the deed must have been done some time back. But why were no scavengers eating the flesh?

When Moogi caught up she looked hard at the body, noticing it was decomposing, and said nothing. Amu wanted to poke it with a long stick.

'Toma kill him?' asked Joha.

'No,' said Moogi emphatically. What was the use of giving Joha hope of catching up with his son along the way? It was so long since he had been gone. 'Bad fuzimo,' she said. 'We look.'

'We go, we look,' replied Joha, then realising Amu had managed to wander off unobserved and was a distance in front, ran as fast as he could after her, his long legs stretched like a cheetah's, fearful of what might spring from the thickets to carry her away. Meanwhile Moogi, equally afraid for her safety, shrieked for Amu to wait for them.

Joha picked her up, put her on his shoulders, told her to keep an eye open for fuzimo, and marched on with Moogi trying to keep up. She thought him a changed male: uncaring of the fact that the stride of his legs measured twice hers. It was only in their shelter at night that he turned to her for comfort in his sorrow, fetching her hand to his ora and accepting her arousal of him by gently mating. During the day's walk he became morose again so that they exchanged few words.

In contrast, Amu kept her mother amused all day. At their next stop she gave a cry of delight, lunged into the grass and brought to light a small tortoise with a shiny yellow and black shell. Moogi picked a stone, raised her arm to kill it for food, when Amu gave a shriek of distress. She snatched the tortoise from her mother and cuddled it to her chest in imitation of Moogi's frequent loving hugs, then giving her an accusing look stumbled away under the burden, murmuring 'Oma' to her new pet. In this way Amu transferred whatever memory she retained of Toma as a playmate to the tortoise and made good her loss. She tried carrying it at the same time as attempting her short walks, frequently collapsing but still holding on to Oma until her mother was forced to carry the tortoise in her food bag.

Whenever the family took a meal, Oma was returned to ground level and Amu watched enthralled as it quickly found some grass to eat. Then she lay down on her tummy to be face to face with her pet and hand-fed it a blade at a time. Travelling in a food pouch together with dead mice, birds' eggs, leaves and various insects didn't seem to bother the tortoise at all, as it never made any attempt to get out. At night Amu insisted on sleeping with Oma in her nest and if the tortoise wandered during the night, she refused to leave the camp at dawn, struggling and kicking in Joha's arms until he made a search and retrieved the baby tortoise from the surrounding vegetation.

All through each day Amu held conversations with the tortoise as her word store increased. 'You sleep?' she inquired of Oma in the pouch. 'You want food?' At a stop with Oma crawling round slowly, Amu followed similarly, providing it with a commentary of what they had seen on the way. 'Hoka say, "Au-au, au-au!"' imitating the bird's call. 'You see buhu? Aghrrr!'

The savannah, their accustomed terrain, changed imperceptibly when trees grew closer. Eventually they were in a forest where thick undergrowth made it difficult to find a way through. Moogi asked why they could not go back to forage where they could see dangerous buhu sometimes before the buhu noticed them.

'No,' Joha replied and continued hacking a path by beating down on vegetation with his cudgel as though he were attacking an animal. He did not want to tell her about the voice in his head that only that dawn had told him the direction to follow. Moogi in turn noticed how he no longer listened to anything she suggested. Yes, he was a changed male since Toma had left them.

The forest was dark, strange noises intimidating: howls, shrieks, and a continuous high-pitched drone, struck their ears. At times they halted on hearing the snapping of undergrowth. Was it big buhu, they wondered, elephants, rhino, or what? The sunshine to which they were accustomed had become an eerie brightness and Joha's obvious nervousness silenced Moogi and Amu's chat.

Suddenly there was a rush of creatures descending the trees. Black-faced, tail up, they bobbed and curtseyed in front of them, wide-eyed and raising their eyebrows, baring their teeth and going 'Huh, huh, huh!' Amu screaming with fright clutched Joha's leg and Moogi moved closer. He swung his cudgel at the animals and for moments it looked as though they were about to attack. Then the biggest of them turned to flee up a tree, followed by the whole troop.

The encounter made them keep even closer together, especially as it grew darker, until Joha stopped for the night and said they could not sleep on the ground. He chose a tree with strong branches, shinned up and made a lot of noise breaking twigs and rustling leaves. Moogi helped Amu up to her father, finding he was preparing an open nest in which they could sit leaning against some of the main branches.

Night closed in with moonlight filtering sparingly through the leaves. Amu cuddled up in Joha's arms; Moogi found sleep by draping her legs over branches for support; Joha dozed, though intent on keeping watch for his family. He was jerked awake feeling something was looking at him. Straight ahead peering through the leaves was a shadowed face. As he focused to see more clearly, the face vanished as leaves replaced the image. Although there was no name for them he reminded himself of the other things he had seen on waking in the night and surmised the face must be one of them. Don't worry they look, they look, he told himself and dozed off again. However, once more during the night he woke with an unease of something happening. Whitish faces with whitish hair were peering at him through the spaces of the lattice nest he had woven; glinting eyes had black circles round them joined over the nose and ears. He drew in a breath and shrank into twigs and leaves behind him, tightly clutching Amu to his chest. His throat constricted, he was unable to make a sound to wake Moogi. What would he do if these fuzimo attacked them? He could not defend himself while holding Amu, and Moogi would be pushed off the tree. Probably all three of them would fall to their death. He sat frozen in fear waiting for whatever was going to happen.

His next look showed him nothing was there, no faces, only leaves. No sound had been made, the faces were there, next moment gone. It was useless waking Moogi. What was he to tell her when he had no name for his night-time horrors? Instead he remained awake, glaring fearfully around him in the dark until it dawned, when he climbed down, inspected the ground at the foot of the tree and found no trace of disturbance.

The experience made him even more cautious as he slashed and bashed a way through thickets during the day wondering whether the noises of the forest, the strange calls from up above in the treetops, howls sounding like somebody being killed, together with flapping and fluttering, were those of the fuzimo of the night. How could he know?

Later they had a drink and filled their empty gourds at a river, relieved they did not have to lick moisture from leaves increasingly dry as the day wore on.

Emerging into more open country Joha stopped, stood absolutely still and listened intently. The voice that he so often heard in his head was calling, 'Go from water.' He immediately veered, leaving the river at his back. Why he always obeyed the voice he could not have explained. It was compelling and he never questioned it. Neither did Moogi ever ask why he made sudden turns. From childhood she and Toma had followed where Joha led: he was their big leader.

Joha's change of direction led them back among herds of grazers and new sorts of plants, but after Oma had chewed them for some days without dying, the three were prepared to try them.

Joha missed Toma more than ever because it had been so much easier to hunt with three adults, one always seeing to Amu. Moogi had been the most skilled until her pregnancy, though after the child's birth she had regained her running speed, and her targeting when throwing stones had never been better. They now took it in turn to provide flesh, either Joha or Moogi attempting to kill whatever small animal crossed their path.

During one of their rests, Amu asleep lying across Joha's legs, Moogi had a chance to practise her skill when she recognised the shape of a gazelle standing among camouflaging bushes. She picked up a throwing stick and rose, crouching in typical stealth position to stalk it by taking a roundabout route. Joha sat rigidly still not to disturb the animal.

The gazelle was preoccupied with something it saw, heard or smelt in the opposite direction, enabling Moogi to creep nearer, foot-silent, arms and head still, body bent in imitation of a gnarled tree trunk. Joha held his breath, all the muscles of his limbs taut as if he were doing the same.

Near the bushes Moogi ducked lower, bent almost double, throwing stick ready, but the gazelle heard her and leaped from the hide. Moogi rushed after it and gave chase. The animal began zigzagging to throw off the pursuer but Moogi, instead of following, anticipated each move and took the short cut to where it was going to turn. Determined to kill for food she felt elated, almost light-headed with pleasure in the action of the chase. The dust rose, the animal wove this way and that, twisted and turned, making crazy angles between bushes and doubling back. Moogi was there and when she was almost falling over her prey, struck home with her hunting stick into the animal's neck. It stumbled and fell, blood gushing from the wound as Joha came running with Amu to smash his cudgel down on its head.

'You good, you good-good!' he said in admiration, and handing Amu over to her, knelt down to start skinning the buhu, putting the best cuts aside before any other predators arrived to claim the kill.

Amu who was watching with interest suddenly ran back towards their resting place shouting, 'Oma, Oma!' followed by Moogi who retrieved her food bag while the child found her pet. They ate the fresh flesh and took what pieces of meat they could store in the bags, Joha carrying the skin he intended to cut into shape for clean food bags.

His mood improved with the feast of succulent meat he had not eaten for months when they had to be satisfied with scraps cut off rodents and snakes, and that night in the shelter his spirits high, he turned to his female not for comfort but with a driving hunger for sex. The image of her slender figure, her stance to deceive the prey, the skill of chase and success in killing the gazelle for their food so aroused him that when he felt her hand on him, he mounted in a storm of passion. At dawn Moogi's shiny eyes told him how successful his ora had been. They left camp hand in hand, Amu making sure Oma was riding in her mother's pouch.

Taller grass, different varieties of trees and therefore new leaves, flowers and fruits to try out occupied Moogi, while Amu tried to keep up with her mother, remarking about everything that crossed their path: columns of ants, stick insects hardly distinguishable from grass stems, chameleons, and ground and aerial spiders. A tamarind tree was in fruit and mother and daughter stopped to collect its sweet-sour pods.

Joha impatiently ahead again was aware of an absence of sound. He could not hear the other two so far behind nor were there the usual noises of birds chirruping up above, or the grunts, snuffling and rustling of small beasts on the ground. The air was stifling. He turned to see whether his family was catching up and noticed the sky behind the tamarind had turned a brown hardly distinguishable from the land surface. In the distant haze things seemed to be moving. They grew in size and came closer. He discerned a faint roaring sound from the same direction as if a storm were blowing up. Still watching with no idea of what it was, Joha heard the roar increase and made out animals running in his direction. He had seen herds disturbed by predators all escaping in one mad rush and realised the situation could be dangerous.

Shouting a warning in Moogi's direction, he followed it up with an even louder bellow drowned in a thunder of hooves within a cloud of thick dust churned by racing legs. Hastily he climbed the nearest tree just in time as the front-runners of the stampede came by. Swirling sand engulfed him; beneath the branches there was a clatter of innumerable hooves. He spluttered and coughed and when he could open his eyes saw buffalo and rhino rushing by, elephants and giraffe, and between the large beasts smaller ones, gazelles and antelopes, hyenas, wild dogs, and warthogs, some caught in the crush scrabbling onto others' backs to be carried along until they fell off and were trampled underfoot.

Joha climbed higher and clung on to the branches, unable to understand why the animals were stampeding. Where was Moogi? Had she climbed a tree in time and with his child? He tried peering through the haze but could not see anything.

Another sound rose: a rolling deep-throated growl as from a huge creature: the ground began to shake and with it the tree. Joha held on. This was something he had experienced, and with the animals fleeing the thought went through his mind that there must be a fight going on between two giant beasts in the direction from which they had come. An ear-splitting explosion followed, the rocking ground gave way in an avalanche of earth and stones, the tree fell, slid, branches whipped Joha's face, wood splintered and cracked off, animals bellowed and screeched, more dust whirled all around and blotted out the sun, and Joha fought for air.

Coughing and spluttering and spitting to clear his throat, he finally regained his breathing. Entangled in the tree by broken branches, he was lying face down on the trunk that pointed downwards on a very steep slope. Around him there were other fallen trees, rocks, animals, some still sliding and rolling down the slope, some creatures half-buried either by their hindquarters and struggling to free themselves or embedded by their shoulders and heads, jerking convulsively in suffocation.

Another deep roar came from beneath him. The tree and everything around him began to move once more and he clung on to the trunk with arms and legs. Some rocks rolled away together with the half-buried animals. Bushes and clumps of grass came flying past, branches tore loose, and Joha shut his eyes in terror.

When the tree came to a standstill and the noise of things going down-slope decreased, he opened his eyes, seeing loose soil beneath him. Gradually the air cleared but on lifting his head the end of the slope was not in sight. A sound of trickling earth continued for a while so that he did not dare move. Some animals with broken limbs still struggling to stand slid away and disappeared; those that could not move whimpered until death silenced them.

After a while it became quiet and Joha still clinging to the trunk thought about Moogi and Amu. If they had not heard his warning shout, if they had not climbed a tree, they must be dead, or perhaps they were all right and waiting for him. Why was he on such a steep slope? He tried to get up but the tree gave a lurch and he ducked down, afraid the trunk might start sliding... but where to? Where was he? Where were Moogi and Amu? He just could not think at all and shut his eyes again. The sun went down, night descended, and Joha exhausted and completely disorientated fell asleep.

DID THE VOICE KNOW BEST?

Next time the Lady Archaeologist paid the camp one of her periodic visits, meagre finds had set her evening free so that she sat under the extended flysheet, reading by the glare of the electric lamp clamped to one of the main poles. This was a new innovation made possible since the government had donated a generator to the camp.

Baratu waited until he could see she had settled down behind her camptable and came to discuss whatever she wished him to do next day. He was therefore startled when with her usual directness she said, 'Something is wrong with you and I had better know what it is.'

Under the blaze of the white electric light he felt exposed and embarrassed, unable to answer.

'The men report,' she continued relentlessly, 'that you have stopped looking for fossils and seem to be sad.'

It was annoying to hear that his men reported about him behind his back but he remained silent.

'Well, if you won't tell me, I shall sign you off sick and send you back on the next supply flight until you feel better.'

'No!'

'Then what's the matter with you?' It was said with sympathy, the Lady Archaeologist never treated her fossil team as underlings. On the contrary she went out of her way to maintain equality amongst persons with a common interest.

Baratu knew her too well: she was kind, fair, clever but determined, and it was useless to remain silent but at least he could try an evasion. 'Didn't my wife tell you?' he said lamely.

'She hasn't. I contacted her only yesterday to enquire whether she wanted anything brought over for you.'

Desperate not to reveal his worry, Baratu tried one more evasion. 'And she said nothing?'

'If she had I wouldn't be asking you,' answered the Lady softly.

'That's bad, if she didn't say anything it means my brother hasn't got better.'

'I thought he was recovering from his concussion.'

At that moment the light bulb flickered and died. At the same time the whirr of the generator ceased and there was silence.

'Back to basics,' said the Lady switching on her pocket torch, and fetched the old pressure lamp which she began to light. The mantle glowed red, orange, light yellow, and finally reaching the required plumpness turned faintly bluish while she pumped the little fuel tank that served as base.

Although dimmer than the bulb, the lamplight lit up the white in Baratu's eyes and emphasised the Lady's ageing wrinkles like valleys in the setting sun.

'That's better,' she said and poured some sparkling water into two tumblers, handing one to Baratu. 'I always feel really at home by the light of the old lamp. Now what about your brother, he is younger, isn't he?'

'He is the youngest in the family and I'm responsible for him.'

'I see,' said the Lady Archaeologist with sincerity. 'Tell me about him.'

'You know about his concussion and coma after his car accident. Recently a brain scan showed improvement so they stopped feeding him through a tube, gave him sips of water and that invalid food like our maize porridge, but he didn't open his eyes. He was quite silent.'

'It must have been very trying for you.'

'Then they put some flavouring in that porridge and he opened his eyes and said, "I don't like it." Just like that! Suddenly he was okay. So we thought, but we found he had lost all memory of his life in the past. He remembered nothing.'

'That does happen,' said the Lady Archaeologist. 'Sometimes people remember gradually and anyway he does recognise you and everything around him.'

'But if he can't remember the past, half the brain is dead and he must be like some of our hominins with half our brain capacity.'

The Lady Archaeologist looked at him thoughtfully for so long that he shuffled his feet with unease. Then she said, 'I understand your grief in thinking a clever Homo sapiens has regressed to Homo erectus standard. You are so steeped in hominin science, Baratu, that you have begun to think about the world along those lines.'

Baratu sat slouched in his chair, increasingly sad as he unfolded his tale. 'Yes,' he said, 'that's the only job I know, the only knowledge I have.'

They were both silent now, Baratu worrying about the life of his little brother, the Lady Archaeologist thinking of how a little knowledge was a bad thing. How was she to remove his worry?

'Wait,' she said suddenly and holding the lamp by its handle went into the tent. 'Don't go,' she called. When she returned there was a little plastic dome on a base in her hands. 'I remembered seeing this toy behind the old tin trunk the other day, it's one my children must have left behind long ago after a holiday.' She held it up for him to see. White flakes disturbed by movement rained down on a miniature Christmas scene and settled on the base.

Baratu, having never seen anything like it, was fascinated and kept shaking it to see the effect.

'It shows you something about your brother's memory,' said the Lady Archaeologist. 'Memory in the brain may be composed of many little units that get transmitted along threads and deposited in parts of the brain in patterns. Get a bang on the head and the units are disturbed, fly about and when they settle, maybe some of the pattern is lost.'

Baratu kept shaking the toy, causing the white flakes to tumble around until they settled again on the base. 'I see,' he said. 'I understand. Half his brain is not dead, just things disturbed inside and not settling down as before.'

'Exactly! In time the units may settle into the old patterns and people begin to remember their past. Of course sometimes the patterns are lost.'

'Thank you for telling me there is hope for my brother's recovery. I will try to stop my worry. Perhaps I will go out tomorrow and look for fossils.'

Baratu rose and disappeared into the pitch-black night outside the lamp's circle of light.

– – – – – –

The rising sun woke Joha from deep sleep. He was still spread-eagled on his tree and for a few moments did not know why. Limbs stiff from the awkward position and hurting everywhere from cuts and bruises, he tried to move off the trunk but being lodged in loose soil it slid slightly and his muscles stiffened as he tightened his grasp. When he lifted his head carefully to glance around there were still many dead animals lying on the surface or half-buried in the landslide, otherwise as far as he could see the place was littered with debris. Jagged sections of tree trunk, pieces of bark with tunnels made by termites now exposed by having been broken off, torn branches, twigs and leaves, clumps of roots and grass, and rocks all lay about on the steep slope that seemed to have no beginning and no end. The lack of definition and of any familiar feature continued to disorientate him and in addition he felt hungry and thirsty. The food bag was still round his shoulder but almost empty. Where was the nearest water, he wondered. On a slope this steep there could not be any. Questions crowded his mind: where were Moogi and Amu? He tried to recall the moments before the stampede obscured his view. Were they standing near a tree, was Moogi bending down picking up something to eat? Did she hear his shout? He could not recall anything, surely nothing had seemed out of the ordinary at that moment. The thoughts flickered like sheet lightning and there was only one conclusion, they were probably dead. His mind screamed 'No!' and he lay still, trying to decide what he could do.

The heat of the sun increased until thirst gradually took over in importance. Water. He had to find some water. In his line of sight sideways across the terrain, another smashed tree lay in the distance. Something showed in its foliage, perhaps some juicy fruit. He must try getting across to it.

Very slowly he slid off the tree, anchoring his hands and feet in the soil. It shifted slightly making him reach for a branch. When he had steadied himself, he made for a torn trunk protruding from the slope a little way off. Lifting one limb at a time he made his way cautiously sideways towards it and then the further fruit tree. Aware he could start sliding down slope any moment, his fingers were flexed ready to dig deeper into the ground until the soil might settle. With slow progress moving on all fours he finally reached what had looked like a fruit tree and grasped one of the bigger branches. At that moment he drew back in fright. There was a leg entangled in the foliage, a fuzimo's. It did not move.

Joha crouching remained still and watchful, but when it gave no sign of life he dared to lift his head to look at the tangle that had once been the crown of the tree. There was a fuzimo male lying among the broken branches, seemingly dead. His face was covered in dried blood, soil and pieces of bark. Bits of wood and torn leaves lay all over his body but the thong of the food pouch was still round his shoulder. Joha bent to remove it and again drew back. The body was warm. His sudden jerk backwards started the soil round his feet sliding, so that he hastily grabbed a branch with both hands to steady himself. Still the fuzimo gave no sign of life. Perhaps he had just died, but when Joha put his nose near the male's fingers they smelled fresh, not like those of a corpse. The fuzimo was alive and asleep.

As his legs were entangled in the branches, this fuzimo could not get up to hurt him. Therefore Joha, curious that the male had not woken at his touch, began clearing vegetation and dust off the face and then gave a grunt of incredulity. He bent closer, brushed away more debris and exclaimed, 'Toma!'

Could it be Toma?

But it was. He was pitifully thin, scratched, scarred and wounded, entangled in broken branches and had his eyes shut.

'Me Joha, no sleep, me father,' said Joha, stroking Toma's hair as he used to do when his son was small.

Toma did not open his eyes, did not even respond to a gentle shake but he was alive and breathing.

This new and extraordinary situation focused Joha's mind. Thirst, he thought, he is dying of thirst. Where could he find water? If he slid down wherever all the other things had gone, in the hope of seeing a river or spring there was nothing with which to carry water back to Toma. His gourd was smashed and in any case the loose soil would not allow a return climb. Perhaps he could pull Toma free and they could both slide down the slope together but when he tugged at the feet, his own constantly slipped and anyway the big branch lying across his son's body must first be cut. Joha looked for his handaxe in his pouch but it had gone, and there was none in Toma's. There was no way of cutting him free.

An idea came to him: he would push the trunk into sliding down and if he hung on, the tree might come to rest at the bottom, wherever that was. He made his way up to the jagged end to try pushing but the tree was big and the trunk did not budge.

Returning to Toma's side, Joha took what was left of bits of food in the pouches, chewed them into a wad and pressed it on his son's lips but with no success. Feeling utterly defeated he sat on a branch and stared at Toma so thin, sores all over and yet asleep with a peaceful expression in an emaciated scratched face.

The sun passed its zenith, the rays beat down hot and thirst-making, and Joha put his head on his knees because he could not bear to look at Toma dying. He dozed in the oppressive heat, becoming only faintly aware of a rumble before he felt the tree giving way under him. He fell, landing on top of the branch holding Toma's body down and grasped it as the ground began to tremble, setting off a further avalanche of earth, vegetation and stones, together with dead animal bodies. The tree trunk moved sedately at first but then gathered momentum, bumping over objects in its path, slurring sideways, twisting this way and that, while Joha curled his legs round a section of the big branch and desperately clung to it.

The noise of the landslide was tremendous, thundering in Joha's ears and taking away all thought, so that after a while when the trunk came to a halt with a jarring thud and the noise decreased he lay still, bewildered and unable to move. He could still hear the trickle of earth and things landing and rolling until pebbles hit him and he was galvanised into action. The smashed branches allowed him to jump off. At the same time seeing some larger rocks rolling down, he pulled his son free, heaved him over one shoulder and dodging the debris, hastily made his way to clear ground where he could stride away at a faster pace.

The terrain was a vast valley. In the distance a line of green vegetation promised a river course towards which he walked, carrying Toma's emaciated body still over his shoulder. The speed of the extraordinary events, stampede and landslides, the discovery of Toma, his strange sleep, and finding himself suddenly on even ground, left Joha unable to grasp what had happened. He walked unheeding, with only an occasional glance not to miss the line of trees.

At the small stream he held his son's head on his lap to feed him water with a cupped hand. Toma's tongue emerged, licking the moisture on his lips, but he drank with eyes shut and clenched his teeth whenever a chewed wad was offered.

Joha washed him, leaving the congealed blood on his sores and noticed just how thin he was, how battered and bruised. It was a long time since he had run away, so long that Amu was now walking, Joha reminded himself and with that realisation came the thought that he did not know what had happened to her and her mother.

While his son continued the deep sleep in the shade, he foraged food in the green vegetation of the riverbank, broke off a stout slender branch for a weapon and decided to walk along the river course so that water was at hand. Perhaps Toma was sleeping after he had been pursued by fuzimo for many days and would wake suddenly.

Always carrying his son on one shoulder or the other, he walked all that day and many more, giving him water and washing off his urine that ran out of him as if he were a newborn child. The burden became progressively lighter as Toma refused food but did drink and remained 'asleep'.

Each dawn Joha followed his voice, so long unheard that the first time it said, 'Go,' he jumped round thinking it was Toma. Despite the relatively light burden, he grew wearier and weaker with the great effort made each day to start another march, always hampered in foraging or hunting small flesh by the fear that Toma might be killed by predators if left unguarded.

Looking at the now distant wall of earth they had slid down, it was obvious that Moogi and Amu, should they have survived the stampede, were lost to him because he could not climb back up. He knew he was becoming weaker. Would Toma die before he could no longer shoulder him? Without Moogi and Amu, without Toma, what was there for him to do? Exhausted, dispirited and sad, he stumbled on day after day, having to stop and rest more frequently but unable to reach a decision as to whether he should leave his son to the vultures.

At one stop he put Toma down and felt too weary to get himself something to eat from the surrounding vegetation. Not far off a hill obscured his view and large boulders made him wary of lurking predators. Buhu would sense Toma's near-death state and surely would begin stalking him. In his mind Joha could hear the crunching sound made by hyenas devouring dead prey. No, he could not leave his son to them. As he looked about him there was one of them or some sort of animal already hiding among the stones. It kept peering out and then withdrawing in a sly manner. Joha froze, only moving his eyes and curling his fingers round the makeshift hunting stick while he waited for the attack.

When the head appeared again it had no upstanding ears, no elongated muzzle. It was not an animal at all but the face of a child.

Fuzimo! Surely there were adults somewhere? Joha felt even more certain an attack was imminent, possibly a rush of shouting males brandishing weapons. He braced himself. They would kill him and Toma too but he was beyond caring. What could he do single-handed and with a helpless son?

He kept still and after a while the face appeared again. The child looked at him and came out from behind the hiding-place, a very young male, slim and hairy, moving fearlessly towards him but not followed by an adult. He walked to Toma's side, bent down to search his face, and kicked him in the side presumably to wake him. Joha flung out an arm to stop the second kick and looked at the child reproachfully but said nothing. The boy held his gaze, stepped to him, took his hand and tried pulling him up. It was an astonishing act of fearlessness and to humour him Joha rose, but when the boy kept tugging at his hand he hesitated, thinking there must be adults watching from the rocks and if he followed him Toma remained unprotected. The boy then took both his hands, showing some irritation as to why the male did not want to come.

There was only one thing to do. Joha let go, picked Toma up as usual, took the child's hand again to renewed tugs and followed him. Once again the turn of events was so strange that he could only think of a cudgel landing on his head in the next few moments.

He was led to the boulders, round the back and into a cool dark area under an overhang. The place seemed empty, until he put his burden down when a short and wizened fuzimo came forward from a dark corner and ignoring Joha, began examining Toma. The child stood by until both retreated to the back of the cave where they seemed to be in the middle of some activity.

Joha completely puzzled did not know what to think of the situation. Was he supposed to wait for other fuzimo? Perhaps he had been lured to the cave to be killed? Toma as usual was lying where he had put him, flat on his back breathing easily and asleep. Wearily Joha put his head on his knees to try working out what he should do. Had he dozed in his weariness? He did not know. Violent coughing and spluttering alerted him and when he looked at Toma, the old fuzimo was pouring a liquid from an animal horn into his mouth, at the same time pinching Toma's nose between his fingers. Before Joha could jump to his assistance Toma opened his eyes and tried sitting up to get his breath, only to collapse back from weakness into the arms of the old man, while the boy poured water on his face from another horn. Then between them they dragged him against the cave wall where he could sit up.

Apart from his first reaction of coming to his son's assistance, Joha now stood looking from one to the other even more perplexed.

Toma wiped his eyes and nose, spat, looked at his father and said, 'Egh! me want water.' The old man offered him some from a drinking horn and returned to his corner, while the young fuzimo bent down to look at Toma's face enquiringly, sat down beside him and taking his skeletal hand began to trace the bones with his finger.

Astonishment, joy at seeing his son awake, the physical strain of the past days all came together, overwhelming Joha. He could not speak and just wanted to keep looking at Toma who did not appear to be at all confused and merely remarked, 'Bad-bad water.'

Presently the old man brought Joha flesh to eat and water in a horn he stuck into the ground to keep upright. Toma was given something different in a half gourd. While they were still eating, a number of fuzimo began to file silently through the gap in the rocks, small hairy figures carrying hunting sticks, food pouches and bits of dead buhu flung over their shoulders. In the dim light filtering through the gap it was difficult to distinguish males from females, especially since their faces seemed all the same to Joha. One of them brought the makeshift hunting stick he had left when the child pulled at his hands and laid it beside him. This sign of friendliness greatly encouraged Joha. Obviously these fuzimo were not going to kill them, and anyway the old man in reviving Toma had done something Joha regarded as 'good-good'.

The band of fuzimo disappeared into the shadows at the back of the rock shelter as though they had walked through the stone. The old man and child had gone with them, leaving the area empty, not a footprint to be seen. Father and son looked at each other. Joha still taking in Toma's recovery did not know what to say to him.

'Fuzimo go where?' Toma asked without showing any astonishment at seeing his father nor at their being in the rock shelter. He did not even notice his sores and his skeletal condition and behaved as though he had journeyed alongside his father and never been in the long 'sleep'.

Joha however was so utterly spent and in need of rest that when the area turned silent he nodded off.

'We go!' said a voice not in his head but beside him. Toma was shaking him gently and the fuzimo child offered a half gourd of food and a horn filled with water. The light of dawn filtered through the passage to the shelter. Of the rest of the fuzimo there was no sign. After their meal, the child and old man led them out of the cave on a walk along the river to a nearby thicket. Toma kept sitting down and resting, hardly able to move his legs, which necessitated Joha's vigilance and made him even more aware that his son looked like a walking corpse and most astonishingly one that did not seem to notice its own condition.

In the light of day the old fuzimo turned out to be a wizened male with a growth of curly white beard and short head hair. He showed the two his sharply pointed hunting sticks and palm-sized pebbles, each encased in a little net of thin thongs with one left long. The longer pieces were gathered into a knot attached to a much longer thong coiled into a bundle slung over a shoulder. He indicated they would be hunting. Joha, Toma and the child were led to a tree; gestures indicated they should sit and keep quiet.

The old fuzimo stepped away into some long grass, immediately mimicking an antelope first grazing then with elongated neck lifting its head to sniff the air. It bent down again to graze, came up in a nervous manner he indicated by twitching his flank in an astonishing feat of muscle control, and finally showed its alarm by quivering with apprehension, until it leapt away all four limbs off the ground.

The other three sat enthralled watching him. Suddenly he stood up, grasped his weapons, assuming the hunter's role stalking the animal by bending almost double, becoming a thing camouflaged by the shadow of grass stems criss-crossing on his body, or twisting himself to resemble a piece of dried wood or other vegetation, then silently throwing himself down to wriggle snake-like towards the imaginary prey, and all the time testing the air to make sure his scent was not being carried to the animal. After a while he skilfully twirled the long thong of the pebbles and letting go, the missiles flew through the air until the whole lot of pebbles and thongs whipped round the trunk of a tree with a swish and clatter. Emitting a whoop of triumph he bore down upon the tree, piercing the ground beside it with a thrust of his hunting stick. The imaginary prey was dead.

The little fuzimo ran forward laughing and wrenched the hunting weapons from the hands of the old man, who walked back to squat beside Joha and Toma while they watched the child taking its turn. Next Joha not to be outdone did his hunting routine, but not used to the bolas was shown its use by the old fuzimo who, standing next to him, was so small that he could have been felled with a blow.

Many days of hunting with the two fuzimo taught Joha and Toma the use of the new weapon and their unspoken rule that a hunter must get his prey single-handedly. They also learnt never to return with the carcass but to cut up the flesh long before reaching the cave, eating some of it at a trot so that it did not attract scavengers and returning with only a small amount for the others. On the way back, the child ran before them skipping and laughing or leading Toma by the hand as though he still needed assistance despite his body filling out and regaining stamina. They had no contact with the rest of the fuzimo family, so that Joha wondered whether there was another opening to the cave. He also thought that these small males and females might have been frightened by his superior size.

The boy appeared alone one dawn and beckoned Joha and Toma to follow him. Instead of taking the usual hunting route he climbed the hill at the back of the rocks and kept disappearing among the bushes and boulders, only to run back making sure the two were keeping up.

Joha climbing behind his son realised how fit he had become: the sores were healed, his shoulders looked massive and his stride was full of energy. Suddenly Joha's mind was filled with the images of Moogi and Amu. How Moogi would revel in seeing Toma again like this, full of strength, but still without a female, he thought sadly.

On reaching the top they found the boy waiting for them, playing with some pebbles and sticks. The view showed that the river course wound round the hill and they had been brought up a short cut leading down to it.

When the two wanted to walk on, the boy did not get up. Joha and Toma exchanged glances. The boy's action became clear: he would be going back home without them.

Toma plucked some stems and blades of grass and twisted them into replicas of four-legged animals by the method Moogi had taught him when they were children. He moved them about on the ground with defining squeals and grunts as the boy's eyes grew bigger and bigger. Finally unable to contain himself any longer, the little fuzimo gathered them up in his cupped hands smiled at Toma and was gone.

'He good child,' Toma remarked.

'He good-good child,' echoed Joha.

Realising they were now on their own, the two males descended the hill to the watercourse. Without instruction from his voice Joha had no idea in which direction they should walk but Toma took one look at the clear water cascading over rocks.

'We go,' he said and pointing upriver struck out with vigorous strides.

Many dawns later at a rest stop Toma glanced at his father as if he were going to say something but instead lapsed into a long silence. 'Joha,' he said eventually, 'where Moogi? Where Amu?'

Joha had no answer. He did not know. It had been the reason why he had not spoken to Toma about them. Apart from that he could not tell how much of the past Toma had begun to remember.

They continued walking for a while until Toma asked the question more persistently. Still Joha did not reply, pretending he was too busy picking fallen nuts at the foot of a tree.

Further on Joha chased a hare and killed it with a swipe of his hunting stick, leaving Toma to cut it up with the handaxe they had chipped from a river pebble. It had taken many dawns to make the new equipment each now carried.

At the next stop Toma gesticulating agitatedly asked once more, 'Where Moogi, where Amu? You say.'

It was a demand Joha could not ignore and hesitatingly and in his own language he began to tell of the animals running in a mass, the earth shaking, the trees being uprooted, and the landslide.

'Where Moogi? Where Amu?' Toma asked even more urgently.

His father tried to say they must be dead because there had been that terrible moment when he looked back to find they had disappeared from view behind a wall of running animals enveloped in a cloud of dust. But he could not formulate the words, could not make a sound. Instead he put his hands over his face, hiding the grief welling up in him in attempting to answer his son's question. Toma put a comforting hand on his father's shoulder patting it gently.

'Moogi no dead. Amu no dead,' he assured him. They sat in silence for a while until Toma asked, 'Where me?'

It was obvious that he still did not remember leaving his family which made Joha decide to omit this part of the past. Instead he told him of the rescue from the tree trunk and cure by the old fuzimo but still did not mention the many days of carrying him.

Toma seemed satisfied with the curtailed explanation. 'We go,' he said resolutely. 'We find Moogi, we find Amu.'

SURVIVAL

Baratu kept his word and having been persuaded by the Lady Archaeologist that his little brother retained all the brain of a Homo sapiens, felt sufficiently cheered to go fossil prospecting. He had the geologists' diagram of the ancient lakeshore and river. They seemed to see through different eyes. Raised banks, ancient riverbed curving and making oxbow lakes. What did they mean?

However much he strained his eyes he could see nothing but a desert-like terrain, sparse trees and a few dried bushes that made the idea of a lake and river – even though ancient - seem ridiculous.

At a place where the raised beach had been pointed out he sat on a rock, glanced at the paper on his knees and looked into the distance, trying to trace the ancient shore. By now the sun was high, the heat like the breath of a fast running animal and objects had no clear outline in the haze.

He tried concentrating on being still, emptying his mind in case he could hear those whisperings that led to fossil finds but nothing came. Finds did not occur often, that was the fascination of his job. He rose, deciding to walk the contour marked on the paper if he could relate it to the terrain. A few steps on he stopped, looked round and returned to the rock. Something had tripped his thoughts. He sat down again and once more examined the soil round the rock. By his left shoe there was something protruding through the surface, no bigger than a coin.

Baratu took a small trowel from his back pocket and tried loosening the object but there was too much of it buried. Could it be a fossil? He got down on his knees, scraped more soil and blew it away to see what would emerge. It was definitely a bone, not hominin but animal and he was sure it had fossilised. He drew out a pencil from a pocket and marked a cross on his paper. Although the find did not seem important he might as well tell the Lady Archaeologist as she was still in camp.

Days later the Lady Archaeologist had made a quick survey of the site, photographed it, marked out a trench one metre square and the team was digging, scraping, brushing, sieving loose soil, and finding fossils of a medium-sized mammal. It was time to enlarge the hole.

At the long worktable that night and with the help of electric lights – the generator working again - the fossil finds were laid out. There were teeth and fragments of bones and skulls. A few had been chewed, the teeth marks clearly visible but most were so smashed and tiny that they were hardly recognisable, possibly the remains of a meal and subsequent trampling.

After the team had worked at sorting and piecing together what seemed to fit, the next task was to attempt assembling one or more partial skeletons. Murmurs began circulating round the table that the animals had been an early type of hyena, jackal, or mere dog.

'In a way you are all wrong, though in a way one of you is right,' said the Lady Archaeologist after examining the fossil teeth closely. 'I believe we have here the remains of ancestors of a wild dog pack, possibly drowned due to some calamity or having been savaged and scavenged by other predators. If so this would be an important discovery because finds of these animals are rare.'

The men pulled faces of disgust. African wild dogs were the pariahs of the animal world.

'You should not be so prejudiced,' she said. 'The present representatives of this type of creature are in danger of becoming extinct in Africa. It is thought that they somehow split off from other dog-like animals about three million years ago. This in a way is like us insofar as we don't know why hominins split from the ape branch.'

The men fell silent, each occupied with his chosen jigsaw of fragments, until one of them nudged Baratu next to him. 'How is it you are always finding important fossils?'

'It is just luck,' he answered modestly.

'No! We know you are a Christian and don't agree with the old ideas that ancestors look after you but you can't deny they are helping.'

Baratu kept quiet. What could he say when the other man was so near the mark – in a way - without knowing it?

— — — — — —

At the moment when Joha shouted his warning of the approaching stampede of animals, Moogi had finished collecting the tamarind fruits, and with Amu on her hips was about to make an extra effort to catch up with him. The tone of his voice warned her of danger, and looking in all directions she saw the distant dust cloud and in it just visible the legs and heads of animals. As they drew nearer, the clatter of their hooves was an ever increasing and frightening sound. One more look back convinced her only fast action could save them both from being run down. The tamarind had big branches, some bowed towards the ground. She swung Amu up and climbed after her just in time as the beasts came thundering past, engulfing them in dust and starting them off in a fit of coughing. Moogi took Amu in her arms, turned the child's face towards her chest between her breasts and shielded her as best she could with one spare hand over her head and one holding on to a branch. The child kept quite still except for coughing fits, allowing Moogi to sit with Amu on her lap.

In addition to the noise of the stampede there came a rumble, culminating in an ear-splitting 'boom'. The tree juddered and rocked and felt as though it was going to fall; the animals broke into a cacophony of bellows, squeals and roars of terror; Moogi felt dizzy and sick. Amu sobbed, calling for Oha and Oma, while her mother clutched her tightly until she composed herself sufficiently to soothe her daughter with talk of bad-bad beasts far-far away, fighting, shaking the earth, though nothing to be afraid of.

The tree stopped swaying, but still coughing and spitting out dust Moogi had to wait for the end of the stampede before peering through the settling dust for a sign of Joha. Just before the charge he had been walking along a line of trees. Of these there was no sign. Instead, as far as the eye could reach, dead and dying animals littered the ground. Never had she seen so much bloody flesh, so many body parts and such a number of animals writhing in pain, shrieking and gurgling in the throes of death. She wanted to put her hands over her ears and to run from the place.

The uniform terrain of brown soil sparsely covered with yellow grass showed no significant landmark now the trees had vanished, nothing indicated where Joha had been. She shouted his name, drowned out by the animals' noises. It was no use, she had better move on. Wherever Joha was at that moment he would surely follow her tracks, or she might come across his. Descending from the tree she picked Amu off the branch, put her on one hip and began walking away from the scene of devastation as fast as the weight of the child allowed.

With death all round her, Moogi asked herself whether Joha was dead as well. The unexpected events, the stampede, shaking earth, the complete disappearance of her male, confused her mind. She could not focus her thoughts. Go on walking, she told herself. If he is alive he will follow your footprints, and she kept turning round expecting to see him hurrying after her. Reading tracks was easy and when she put Amu down to walk, the slowed pace enabled her to scrutinise the ground for signs of him, as well as choosing the way ahead dictated by vegetation and the lie of the land.

No sooner had they left the tree and the scene of slaughter, when once again there came a booming sound that grew louder and louder. Moogi and Amu threw themselves on the ground fearing something was approaching overhead. The earth trembled, mother and child lay still petrified. The deep roar passed under them and as it receded the ground steadied followed by complete silence.

Oma's scrabbling in the food bag made them realise it needed to graze. Moogi sat up and let him out. Amu was given some tamarind fruits to suck, but being sour she spat them out and asked for her favourite worms to chew.

Whatever made the awful noise, Moogi thought, had gone far away. As before, the earth had shaken, and what terrible beasts these buhu must be who caused such tremors. She shook her head to rid herself of her mind's image showing a creature as large as a nearby hill. But the danger had surely passed. Letting her eyes sweep over the vast surrounding countryside, she noted there was no breeze, no bird in the sky, no animal, nothing stirred. Her world had cowered before the beast.

She was alone with Amu and Oma, glad of the food pouch with her handaxe still in it, pleased she had picked up the hunting stick dropped when she climbed the tamarind. She would keep the sun on the side that it had been when Joha called to her. If he was still alive he would surely catch up with them with his fast gait.

Hungry now, she was sorry not to have cut flesh off those many dead animals. There was plenty of fluid in her breasts for Amu but for herself she must find water to fill the gourd, and the child would have to do more walking until Joha caught up with them. Having decided on a course of action, Moogi put Oma back in the pouch slung over one shoulder, heaved Amu onto the other hip, and with the hunting stick for support marched slowly on.

Next day the ground under them moved again but only slightly while they were at rest and Amu asleep, but with no animals in sight Moogi did not have to worry about their reaction. She continued their walk afterwards, choosing open grassland for safety where she could see any approaching danger and where they would be visible to Joha who was surely somewhere behind running to reach them.

Plants with tubers kept her thirst at bay, insects, and rodents killed with a swipe of her stick provided food, though it was a meagre diet. Although she longed to hunt bigger flesh, there was no way Amu could be left unprotected for even a moment. The memory of all those fleeing animals with predators in their midst was still too vivid in her mind. Fortunately Amu's legs grew stronger with each day, enabling her to walk a little further before raising her arms to beg for a lift.

At sundown Moogi chose a tree or bush from which to break branches for construction of the nightly shelter, aided by Amu who had learnt what to do and helped by holding the planted sticks for her mother to intertwine them into a gwa. They both pulled up tufts of grass for bedding, after which Oma was allowed out of the pouch and after happy reunion with her playmate, Amu was prepared to shut her eyes in sleep.

Moogi often lay awake longing for Joha, grieving that he must have died since he had not caught up with them and wondering how she could keep going with Amu, who was increasingly heavy yet could not walk unassisted for a whole day.

The child was a companion in loneliness. She was just beginning to string words together, trying hard to express herself in the excited and lively manner of her mother.

'Oogi,' she said, 'me want …'

Moogi stopped in her tracks and looked questioningly at her daughter.

'Me want aaaaaah,' and she gestured, pulling something from the ground while making 'aghh' and 'eeeh' sounds of exertion.

Moogi understood. Amu was fond of chewing the very long worms sometimes found in loose soil near water. Shorter ones would have to do for now.

'Oogi, me want Oma,' she said one late afternoon as daylight was turning to dusk, searching frantically for her pet in some nearby vegetation. Moogi always hoped the tortoise would get lost as it had grown somewhat larger and heavier to carry. She made a feeble and unsuccessful attempt to find it.

'Oogi no look for Oma, Oogi look for frogs,' Amu said sternly and retrieved the tortoise from a clump of grass, tossing her head in triumph. She had grown into a very sturdy girl, taking after Joha's build, and seemed to be sure of things beyond her understanding.

One day when they were resting in a shady spot, Moogi, tired out and unable to think of what to do next without her male, could not stop her tears, while Amu was giving her pet a running commentary of their morning's walk.

Suddenly she turned to her mother and said, 'No cry, Joha there, Oma there!' She pointed in a direction.

'Where?' Moogi shook her daughter. 'Where Joha?'

But Amu looked away, went on playing with the pet and asked it, 'You want aaaaaah?'

Moogi decided there and then she must stop longing for her male. He was dead but his child lived and if it was not to suffer death from a predator, she must find some fuzimo who might allow them to join their group. She knew what that would mean: one of the males would probably want to mate with her. Joha had been so kind and yet exciting in sex that the image of another male and strange ora struck her with terror. She looked around furtively, already fearing a meeting with a fuzimo and yet desperately wishing one would turn up.

'We go,' she said, put Oma in her pouch and led Amu by the hand. Slowly the two walked across the wide expanse of savannah, lonely and unprotected.

Later in the day as if in answer to her decision, a large group of fuzimo became visible in the distance. They were resting in the shade of trees Moogi had been walking towards in the hope of finding water. She approached cautiously. They were milling about, some climbing trees, perhaps searching for fruit or nuts. Would they be friendly or might they come at her with cudgels? Quickly she ducked down and took Amu into some tall grass that hid them completely. Should she show herself or try to get nearer by means of creeping through the vegetation? Her whole being screamed against revealing herself, a highly dangerous act, but she must find strength in numbers. Continuing to forage and walk in the hope of finding Joha no longer made sense.

She cautioned her daughter to be silent but the child, used to sudden dangers, always adopted her mother's stance. They began moving sideways through the stems, causing no more stir than a breeze would have done. Strange sounds reached their ears, squeals and grunts, the swish of leaves being torn from branches, a smacking of lips, feet running this way and that. Moogi, almost bent double, hands held close to body, drew nearer slowly, trying to get a view of what was going on. Suddenly there was a screech of alarm and successive barking sounds followed by a rush off the trees

Looking up she realised the fuzimo in the branches had seen them from above. Warning calls mingling with aggressive roars made Moogi stand up to look, hunting stick ready. The group were galloping away on all fours, infants clinging to their mothers' hairy bodies.

'Fuzimo?' she queried to no one in particular since Amu from her position lower in the grass could not see them. Fuzimo that ran like animals? She felt confused and longed to have Joha and Toma beside her. They might have had an explanation, but it was useless to think of her males she reminded herself, both now lost to her. Rather it was a warning not to walk openly towards fuzimo who might turn out to be buhu. She stepped from the grass cover now the creatures had vanished over a rise and the two continued on their way, finding a stream the other side of the trees but no trace of the troop.

Mother and child travelled dawn after dawn without ever coming across Joha's trail. Moogi continued to mourn for him, wishing he could hear his child now clearly pronouncing 'Joha' and 'Toma', and walking all day without help. Amu increasingly aware of her environment was proving to be a fast learner so that she was almost gathering enough to feed herself. Though still so young she emulated Moogi in killing small flesh using a little hunting stick made for her; she chipped stones to try producing a handaxe when Moogi made herself a new one, talked all day and even piped up with her small voice when Moogi felt like singing. She learnt to avoid snakes, scorpions and tarantulas, and was adept at raiding nests, handling the eggs carefully as she carried them to her mother. Long-armed and long-legged, she had a dusky complexion, short brown to reddish strong hair, and Moogi's liveliness. Oma continued to be her pet to which she confided her thoughts, worries and pleasures: 'Moogi cross, Moogi no like you. Me like you.'

Moogi had to listen to the prattle since she could never be far from her daughter's side. One evening she heard Amu saying, 'Oma, you see Joha? There. You see Toma? There, walking.' It was sad to hear her child still believing her father to be alive, even though she had tried telling her he was dead. Amu refused to listen and at such moments ignored her mother and turned to the tortoise. 'You good buhu, you hear Amu, Moogi no hear.' She cheered Moogi into finding the will to go on looking for friendly fuzimo in a countryside where danger could threaten at a moment's notice.

One day a movement in the distance turned out to be animals, hyena-size but without their typical outline of sloping backs. Moogi always made sure there would be no encounter and this time she became doubly afraid when she recognised the large triangular upstanding ears of wild dogs. Joha had always maintained they were the most dangerous buhu, far more so than leopards, lions, cheetahs or hyenas.

She changed direction, keeping an eye on the animals but soon realised they were doing the same and probably stalking her and Amu. Where was the nearest tree? Wild dogs unlike some predators did not climb.

'We go quick,' she commanded Amu and taking her hand ran dragging her to the nearest tree, another stout tamarind. She helped Amu climb up and followed, still carrying the pouch across a shoulder, gourd tied to it by a thong, clutching her hunting stick and hoping the animals were off to somewhere else.

There had been no rain for a while; the vegetation still showed yellow on brown soil. Moogi looking between the branches commanded an all-round view. Below her she caught a flicker of movement as the dogs crept up flat on their bellies, their colouring perfectly matching dry grass and darker earth, and only becoming visible when they stopped in the greener vegetation growing in the shade of the tree. She and Amu were trapped after all, for as she knew they were ready to close in for a kill the moment she descended. This was their hunting skill, the tactic of surrounding an animal, bringing it down by grabbing it round the legs and in concerted action biting it to death. There was no way out for her and Amu but to sit in the tree until the pack left.

Apart from Oma there was food in the pouch, Amu was still suckling and the gourd was full. Moogi sat on the branch in the most comfortable position with Amu on her lap and hoped the animals would grow tired of waiting.

The sun moved down the sky, set, darkness quickly hid all objects so that Moogi no longer knew whether the wild dogs were still there or not. She leaned against the main trunk, legs stretched on the branch. After feeding Amu from the pouch and taking food herself, the thongs were tied so Oma could not crawl out. The hunting stick was placed between forked branches, and holding the sleeping Amu firmly against her Moogi prepared to stay awake all night hoping she would not fall off. Perhaps the animals would tire of waiting for their prey; maybe dawn would show they had gone.

Night noises set in: night birds called, lions roared in the distance, bats flitted about, a breeze rattled the dry leaves, hyenas making their laughter-like calls were answered by others. These familiar sounds made Moogi sleepy. How she wished she were in her usual night-time gwa of thorny acacia branches.

To keep herself awake she sang in her head, words of misery, words lamenting her mate's death, words of hope that Toma was still alive and lastly words to give her courage to protect her child. Sometimes she talked silently to Joha or Toma as though they were sitting on branches above her.

Dawn lit up the land rapidly. Amu woke and passed urine; Oma scrabbled to be let out. Moogi who had shuffled into different positions all night moved to get a view of the ground under the tree. The animals were there: some, nose on paw, eyed her, others lay stretched out asleep. The pack sentries were on alert. Moogi became anxious, wondering how long the dogs might remain in one place to flush out a quarry.

As there was no need for silence the pair spent the day talking and eating what Oma had left them in the pouch, Amu suckled milk and her mother worried. Holding Amu safely on her lap was tiring her out. How long could she balance on the branch without falling asleep?

During periods when Amu slept, Moogi watched the animals, noticing how some of the pack slunk away always leaving enough of their number for an easy kill. Every time she moved they pricked up their ears, raised their heads, and watched. If only she had Joha with her. Joha was so big, and of course so had Toma been. They would have warded off the dogs with menacing shouts and would have beaten them off with their sticks, but as she was so much smaller and Amu a child, the dogs must surely regard them as bite-size.

'Big!' Yes, if only she could look big, they might be frightened off. Moogi began thinking of ways to appear bigger but every plan she made had the drawback that the dogs would recognise Amu as small and helpless and therefore an easy prey.

The tamarind was old and the branches stout but sitting on one spot was cramping, and keeping her balance even more difficult while holding Amu away from herself so she could pass urine and turds, and sometimes having to do the same for herself still holding on to Amu.

They spent another day talking and sometimes singing since it made no difference to the pack below. They played a finger game: four fingers was a very big buhu, two stood for a small buhu, one for a hoka, and three for an unknown. Both of them on Moogi's command held out the number of fingers of their choice and said the name of that creature. If both hands showed the same number of fingers the outcome depended on the fierceness of the animal named. Moogi made up all sorts attributes but Amu merely said, 'Bi-i-ig, ba-a-ad buhu,' or, 'Big, bad hoka,' with a fierce face that made them both laugh and her mother let her win. Sometimes Moogi told simple tales using her fingers to act, which made Amu copy her mother. At one stage she was concerned about Oma. 'He want out,' she said reaching for the pouch.

Moogi stopped her with, 'Oma now sleep.' After much scrabbling the tortoise gave up, became quiet and was not heard again. Moogi suspected it dead. Amu however frequently grew impatient and begged, 'Me want go.' Especially when a glance down made her think the animals had left.

Even when the large shadow of the tree darkened the area around and made the place look deserted, Moogi knew the dogs were somewhere near, indistinguishable from the dry grass into which they moved from time to time to lure their prey down.

There was sudden excitement below when a herd of buffalo grazed nearby and the leader of the pack streaked towards them followed by a number of others close behind. Moogi took up the pouch and stick, told Amu to hang on to her with arms round her neck, and prepared to descend. But after her first few movements the guards closed in at the bottom of the tree, waiting to catch their quarry, forcing Moogi to retreat.

Meanwhile the other dogs had caught one of the buffalo calves, despite furious milling around by the herd and individuals trying to defend it by running head down to gore the enemy with their huge horns. The dogs hung on to the calf, dragged it down and suffocated it by biting its throat and snout. Amu watched with fascination in her mother's safe arms but Moogi averted her eyes, seeing the same fate for her own young one should she attempt to descend.

The dogs dragged the dead calf to the tree, where the pack busied itself tearing its flesh off and crunching the bones. Moogi made another attempt to descend while their attention was occupied but no sooner had she placed a foot on a lower branch than they looked up, snarled and some moved nearer to keep an eye on her.

The sun passed overhead, the air was hot but the tree afforded shade to hunters and hunted alike. The dogs, satiated, lay in the grass, only their big ears twitching this way and that to catch every sound of movement their cornered prey was making up above.

Since Amu had seen them tearing the calf apart she had become quiet, demanding nothing and cowering into her mother's breasts. The sun set once more and when darkness came Moogi realised their only hope was in her staying awake another night holding Amu. With sickening certainty she also knew it was her last; she could not hold out much longer because she felt increasingly sleepy.

There were short sharp barks from below in answer to a hyena's nearby call, again the lions grunted and roared, a leopard made its coughing noises somewhere in the vicinity, the night birds fluttered above and the bats dashed about in pursuit of insects. Moogi shifted this way and that to stay awake, one arm round Amu, a hand holding on to a branch, her mind desperately thinking of a solution. A crescent moon shed a little light on the land. Frogs croaked; there must be water near, Moogi noted.

Over and over again she thought of how she could climb down leaving Amu in the fork. She would club as many dogs as attacked her. She saw them all lying dead. No, it was impossible, there were too many and sooner or later she would be dragged down and killed.

The night wore on. Moogi thinking out escape plans did not feel sleepy. At dawn she looked down: the dogs had not moved but she was ready to act.

After feeding Amu she began breaking off branches and twigs within reach and placed them where she had put her stick between two lesser forks. This was a difficult task because she had to hold the child at the same time. Then she instructed Amu about what they were going to do, not once but many times until the child completed her sentences because she knew which words came next.

Moogi made crowns of intertwined twigs and leaves to fit on their heads, and throwing the pouch over her shoulder with its thong running across her chest, stuck branches between it and her body so that they stuck up on either side of her head. Amu meanwhile sat on the main trunk, holding on to another branch while Moogi let herself down very slowly to stand on a lower one. Amu sure-footed and without hesitation moved onto her shoulder, feet dangling in front and hands round her mother's forehead and the leaf crown, in imitation of the way Joha used to carry her. Longer twigs were placed between Amu's toes so that they also went past on either side of Moogi's head but inside the child's clasping arms. More twigs had been placed between Moogi's own toes and she took two long leafy ones between her teeth so that they stuck out in opposite directions like a leafy cat's whisker. Lastly she held a branch in one hand and another together with her hunting stick in the other.

Completing the disguise was slow work. Branches had to be trimmed, twigs fell off and had to be replaced, and Amu got tired, slackened her back causing things to slip which then had to be repositioned. The dogs looked up now and then but as the activity continued they lost interest. Snout on paw they slept in the midday heat, relying on their large ears to catch the sound of any change in movement from above.

The apparition, spiky, silent, stood on a branch and began descending at snail's pace, stopping, letting itself down to the next branch, halting, straightening to look erect and tall, coming down again four-eyed and leaf-covered. The nearest dogs lifted their heads, looked up, growled and shuffled backwards. The pack stirred, not sure whether what was moving down the tree was edible, and being belly-full they were no longer interested. Those further off began slinking away. The strange creature continued to descend, huge, unrecognisable, and suddenly the whole pack turned tail and bolted across the savannah into the distance.

THE FUZIMO

After a scorching day the air rapidly cooled to feel almost chilly and the campfire was lit to provide warmth and a focal point for the fossil team. Some retired with a radio for company but others sat or lay near the heat, and once the flames had been reduced to glowing embers, stuck a maize cob or sweet potato under the hot ashes for a late snack. A delicious smell of the half-charred food filled the air.

Baratu joined the fossil team for an evening cigarette and sat in silence, watching a huge full moon rising over the horizon, gradually reverting to its normal shape. It lit up the landscape while the fire played light and dark on the men's brown faces.

'Our fossils must have seen this same moon,' he remarked conversationally.

'Those apes? never!' replied one of the team.

'Well, the apes-becoming-men.'

'No, not even the Australopithecines would have noticed the moon, not enough…'

Baratu interrupted. 'Wait! We've dug up hominins with braincases of 800-900 cc capacity.'

'My cousin should have at least 1400 cc but I don't think he's ever looked at the moon, even when eclipsed,' said another man.

Someone else added, 'There are very old stories about the moon, probably coming from long long ago. I've heard it said that at the beginning of the earth, the moon sent a hare to tell people they would live for ever, just like it dies at dawn but rises again at night. The hare couldn't remember what the moon said and told everybody they would die some time like the moon at dawn, never to rise again. So people believed it and now can't live for ever.'

'You're right about these old stories, they must belong to another time,' agreed Baratu. 'My people used to believe the moon is the wife of the sun. They quarrelled, the sun beat her and she now has scratches all over her face.'

'My people used to believe the bright star next to the moon helps it to shine so night-time travellers can see better,' said another.

They all looked up at the moon to observe.

'I still think the hominins noticed it and probably had their own ideas about it,' Baratu concluded.

– – – – – –

The tortoise Oma was not dead, but crept out hesitatingly the next time Moogi opened the food pouch after she and Amu had managed to descend from the tree in their escape from the wild dogs. Amu was overjoyed at being reunited with her pet.

'Bad buhu, arrgh,' she imitated the dogs. 'Moogi, Amu, make big buhu.' She puffed herself up and stood tall, then knelt down to Oma hungrily chewing grass. 'Moogi put tree here, here, here,' showing the tortoise where her mother had placed the twigs and branches on her. 'Buhu run, run, oooy!'

Moogi had to smile at her daughter's descriptions but then looked round about her fearfully, wondering whether the animals had followed. There was no sign of them. Joha was not going to turn up to guard her and the child from marauding buhu, she told herself as so many times before, therefore they must find some friendly fuzimo for their safety. She had found the river the frogs' croaking had led her to believe was near, and if they continued along its course, there might be a chance of meeting fuzimo also in need of water.

The small female and child walked dawn after dawn, foraging for food on their way. Moogi climbed trees to pluck the few remaining tender leaves for Amu, dug tubers for a hard-to-chew but tummy-filling meal and avoided the river only when animals were trotting down to drink. To stop herself from thinking about Joha she constantly talked or sang to Amu, who responded by adding words of her own.

When Moogi sang, 'We go river, we get water,' Amu added, 'We get frogs, we get frogs.'

At sunset when they made their safety shelter from branches of thorn bushes, it was an opportunity to teach her child to be observant. There might be a bad-bad snake slithering up a stem or a predator might be hidden in undergrowth nearby. One day her teaching bore fruit: Amu called to her mother urgently to come and see. Near a streambed and in the shade of a small tree there were tufts of grass growing lopsidedly. A closer look made Moogi gasp. They were not growing at all but had been placed, root, stem and leaf, on thin boughs spanning a deep hole, a trap for animals to fall into on the trail to the water.

'Fuzimo!' exclaimed Moogi. 'Where feet?' She examined the area for footprints but found none. 'We stay,' she said resolutely. This was a chance to meet one or more strangers and she had to take it. They sat on the other side of the tree in its shade, let Oma out and waited but nobody came. That night they made their shelter nearby and at dawn when Amu asked, 'We go?' Moogi stuck by her decision, repeating, 'We stay.'

During the day they foraged for food, never straying far from the trap. Amu found birds' eggs and Moogi killed a young hare not old enough to know danger. She was butchering it when Amu said, 'He come.' Moogi ducked down and peered into the distance obscured by heat haze but failed to see anything unusual.

After a while Amu repeated, 'He come!' and flattened herself on the ground.

Moogi, doing the same, raised her head slightly to look around but still saw nothing alive approaching.

When her mother made to rise, Amu pulled her down, whispering, 'He come, he come.'

They lay flat in the grass, Moogi in two minds about believing the young child. Presently there was a sound of grass trodden underfoot. She peered through the vegetation and to her astonishment a fuzimo was bending over the trap. It was a light-coloured lanky male with long dark hair, which gave Moogi a shock when she realised he looked like her own reflection in river water. Feeling no apprehension, she stood up slowly not to frighten him and walked cautiously round the tree into the open.

The male in turn gave no sign of astonishment. 'You stay for me?' he asked, while inspecting the trap.

It was speech she understood. 'Yes.'

Without taking further notice of her, he placed a few more tufts of grass on the boughs and said, 'We go.'

Moogi was puzzled. She had expected astonishment even aggression, though she had hoped he would not hit her over the head. Anything would have been easier to understand than this male's instant acceptance of her presence.

'Me have child,' she said lamely. He took no notice and began walking away.

'Amu,' shouted Moogi, suddenly afraid she was going to lose this fuzimo, 'we go.' But Amu had already collected Oma, the pouch and their sticks and was coming round the tree.

Seeing her the fuzimo stopped, looked from one to the other, at last showing interest. 'Child from you?' he asked disbelievingly.

'Yes,' Moogi put an arm defensively round Amu.

The male looked away. 'We go,' he repeated and walked off at a fast pace which they tried to follow by jogging behind him.

Moogi, making sure Amu kept up, revised the preceding events in her mind: we meet fuzimo, he look like me, he no want to kill me, he say, 'You stay for me?' he say, 'We go.' She could not make it out at all. How could he think she was waiting for him? But just as strange was Amu's knowledge. 'He come,' she had said with certainty when there was nobody to be seen. How did she know he was approaching?

Glancing at Amu she saw the child was out of breath in her effort to keep up. Nevertheless Amu suddenly dashed forward, and drawing level with the fuzimo, she told him, 'Me - eh - Amu,' obviously in the hope of attracting his attention.

He jumped with fright, stepped sideways and looked round pleadingly at Moogi, who understood he meant, 'Keep her away from me.' She called

Amu back and wondered how a big fuzimo could be frightened of something so much smaller.

His pace did not slacken and Moogi did not dare ask whether he could slow down for her child's sake in case he decided to abandon them for not keeping up with him. So she took Amu's hand and lifted her over grass and stones as though they were playing a game. The child's legs were sturdy and she loved running and jumping, so much so that Moogi was glad the fuzimo never looked back to see Amu's antics which might have frightened him again.

It was sunset when he stopped. 'Me go,' he informed them. 'Say to others,' and he motioned them to sit while he disappeared into a grove of trees.

They sat as told and waited for his family to allow them to come but nobody turned up. Darkness descended so rapidly that they were soon bathed in the light of a waning moon. Moogi broke off a few branches from the trees with which to make a flimsy shelter for their safety without having time to gather grass for bedding. They lay down on the warm earth and exhausted immediately went to sleep.

Moogi rose at sunrise, sad that her hopes of finding friendly fuzimo had been dashed. Amu placed Oma in their food pouch and they continued on their way along the stream. Amu skipped in front, pulling, plucking, running back and forth to stuff her harvest into the overflowing pouch, but Moogi could not raise her own spirits. The chance she had hoped for had passed and for the first time her courage drained away. She dragged herself along, not listening to Amu's talk, her exclamations, her urges to go faster, and when the heat was stifling pulled her daughter down in the shade of a tree to be quiet and rest. At that moment figures rose out of the tall grass and they were surrounded by fuzimo.

Moogi stifled a cry. Frightened and apprehensive of their possible reaction to her child she at once put her arms round Amu who was pressing into her mother's side, both sitting still, waiting for what would happen next. The strangers approached cautiously, trying to peer at Amu over whom Moogi bent to shield her from a possible blow with a cudgel. One by one they turned away and disappeared into the tall grass as silently as they had come.

When nothing further happened, Moogi pulled her daughter up, they took their belongings and hastily left the shade but no sooner had they started walking than the strangers once more appeared and herded them along. It was all done in silence but not threateningly and as they resembled the male from the previous day, Moogi thought they might be friendly if she spoke to them in an inoffensive way.

'Child want water,' she told the nearest one.

This drew no response. The horde continued walking, always keeping the two in their midst until at last they reached a grove of trees with scattered shelters.

Several children came running, immediately pulling on Amu's hands to join them in play. A female brought water in a gourd and a male handed Moogi some chunks of meat. She understood they had accepted her because she looked like them but what of Amu? The way they had peered at her showed their curiosity about her looks. The huge relief she felt was tinged with worry. Were these fuzimo also frightened of Amu, would they harm her? Would they allow them both to stay?

As days passed and the grown-ups took little notice of Amu, Moogi was grateful for being allowed to remain in the safety of numbers. At first, starved of adult company, she wanted to talk to them, to tell them about Toma, bewail Joha's probable death and relate her adventures after the stampede, but despite their generous supply of food they seemed so indifferent to her presence that she felt gagged, especially since they did not talk much among themselves. Their laughter was scarce; they did not sing. The females went off at dawn to forage leaving a few of their number to look after babies and young children, and some males guarded the camp. Other males disappeared sometimes for many dawns, returning with flesh for everybody to eat.

Of children there were few, all soon following Amu everywhere to enjoy her inventive games, tumbling over each other, skipping round trees and suddenly crouching quite still, only to jump up with a shout as an element of surprise to frighten the others. They traced patterns in the soil with fingers or lined up leaves and twigs in rows and other shapes that Moogi taught them. They played with Oma, prattled as much as Amu and copied her when she whittled little hunting sticks and showed them how to try and hit a target. From her too they learnt to accompany simple tales with fingers acting out the drama, though Amu's stories went on for longer:

'The buhu say arrrrgh, we run,

Oma not run.

We take Oma up tree,

The buhu say arrrrgh to Oma.

Oma say sweeee.

Moogi put branches on me, put me on shoulder,

Buhu run, run, run, eba, eba, eba!

We come down from tree.'

Amu walked taller than the rest, faster, was always laughing yet caring if one of them was hurt, when she would run to Moogi for help to soothe her friend's pain. She loved water when there was more flow in the nearby stream so that she could wallow in it watched by her mother for safety, and one day when they observed elephants downstream rolling in mud, Amu wanted to besmear herself the same way.

Moogi thought the fuzimo strange in behaviour. Mothers returning from foraging were met by the children running to beg for titbits, but when the males returned, the children took no notice. At first she had gone with the females to learn what they thought edible, sometimes plants and roots she had never eaten. She helped them collect termites that they dug up laboriously with digging sticks stuck into anthills whereas she could swipe it with her handaxe, sending the clods flying. The females eyed the implement with curiosity since their males only made scrapers used in butchering. Al the fuzimo made use of gourds growing in profusion all over the surrounding area. Dried and scraped they served for fetching water or transporting small edibles, while larger plants or tubers were tied with thongs made by the males from animal skins and were carried by means of a loop.

When it rained and the savannah greened, the females hardly had anything to do as the food grew almost up to the door of their shelters but in the dry or drought seasons they walked far to forage, keeping together, a silent group of fuzimo who ran home at the slightest sign of danger.

One day a rush of them arrived back panting and frightened, almost incoherent, all pointing at something. Moogi had stayed in camp with Amu and her friends and when she looked in the indicated direction there were small animals running up and down trees, gathering fruits, and some sitting on the ground eating. They were similar to the ones that had frightened even Joha when they had travelled through the forest. The fuzimo guards after one glance took no further notice, while the fuzimo females, still cowering in a group, kept looking at the males to do something. Moogi noticed the lack of communication between the sexes. Very few words were ever exchanged and the males like their females hardly talked among themselves.

Every few dawns these males gathered to decide whose turn it was to remain behind as guards. Agreement was reached before many words were exchanged if any, sending a number of them marching off to hunt. On their return, shouldering carcasses of flesh, the males cut the meat into strips, wrapped them in leaves and hung them from trees by bark fibres to dry in the sun.

Those men not sent to hunt filled in their time by knapping stone scrapers, whittling sticks, shaving bark off new cudgels and digging sticks and sharpening the tips by means of discarded stone chips.

At sunset the strips of meat were always taken into the shelters for fear that predators would eat them during the night. Following the example of the others, Moogi and Amu learnt to keep a dried strip dangling from the mouth while they slowly chewed on the sun-hardened flesh until a section was soft enough to bite off and swallow.

At times when all the males were home Moogi observed that once darkness fell, they and all the grown females emerged from their shelters, paired up and mated among the trees. She could not make out whether the same male and female went off together or whether they paired at random, but the noise made was unmistakable. She remembered her own copulation with Joha, and his expressions and her responses. From every corner of the encampment came grunts and squeals, sometimes accompanied by an extra bellow or shriek. Were these meant to be pleasure?

At dusk all the children were called to their shelters for safety. When Moogi bedded Amu and Oma down for the night her worries began: might she be asked to join in the adults' activities? Would she have to submit to a male? She lay in the shelter remembering the desire she experienced to stimulate Joha, the relief when his ora entered her, his urgency in love, the weight of his big body he was always careful to keep off her until he mounted in excitement, and she tried to relive it all rather than listening to what others were doing outside. Were they not afraid of danger in the dark, or were there sentries posted all round? She remembered how Toma had stood guard for her and Joha.

The land was bright with moonlight one night when Moogi woke and crawled from her grassy sleeping-place to relieve herself. Always aware of danger from concealed predators, she emerged cautiously, peering about. The shelters scattered under trees in the glade were never silent: grunts and snores, children's sleepy whimpers or cries, became part of the night's crop of animal calls further off, the roar of a lion, more frequently the hysterical laugh of a hyena or yap of a jackal, the chirp of a night bird.

Slight crunching noises, a disturbance of dry leaves froze her into inaction. A figure left a shelter to step into the open. The fuzimo males in contrast to their females tended to move with characteristic fast gait. This one seemed half asleep and she watched with astonishment when he put his hands in front as if feeling the way and walked slowly up a slight rise nearby. On top he was silhouetted against the starry sky and sheen of the moon.

As she watched she became aware that his figure was fading into the background. The night had become darker and continued to darken until the figure was no longer visible. Moogi looked on in astonishment: everything around her was now cloaked in darkness. She glanced once more in the direction of the hill, and looking up saw the moon cut in half and glowing only dimly.

Her surroundings had become quiet, the night noises ceased. She was intrigued, where had the male gone? Why was it suddenly so dark? And so quiet? She sat down outside the gwa to watch. The moon did not remain the same, the colour changed. She knew in her mind it had changed but she had no name for what she saw except that it was a bit like blood from a buhu. That made her frightened, remembering the blood shooting up from the mountain, the earth shaking under her feet. She hoped fervently there were no buhu up there fighting and losing blood, and she watched with fascination the moon turning a deeper shade. There must be buhu up there after all. Strange she had never noticed any. Maybe though – yes – perhaps all the dots in the night sky were eyes. Eyes of the many buhu of which two were fighting right now.

Having given herself an explanation she felt calmer but determined to watch the outcome of what could be going on above.

She was almost dozing off when she noticed moonlight once more gleaming on her surroundings, and looking up, there was that buhu shining fully as on many previous nights. The fuzimo was visible again on the hill. Suddenly he let out a terrible cry that reverberated in the silent night, raised his arms towards the buhu and either fell or threw himself over the hill crest. Moogi stood up shocked. His cry had been so alarming and his action so vehement that she wanted to run to his aid. No, she cautioned herself, the fuzimo were not really friendly, she had better not go to see what had happened to him, especially as nobody had stirred in the camp. She crawled into her gwa tired and bewildered.

What could it all mean? How strange these fuzimo were with their nightly mating and children who seemed to have no fathers. Why did they never exchange more than a few words with her and each other? Amu knew more words than they did and her cheery chat continued all day. Why were the females so tongue-tied? The males were no different, preparing flesh and skins, guarding the camp, always in silence. What was the connection between the male on the hill and the buhu in the sky? Finding no answers Moogi went to sleep.

From next day onwards she felt increasingly depressed by the fuzimo indifference towards her, the monotony of picking leaves, the absence of those long-distance walks, and lack of excitement that hunting with her males once provided. She decided to go her own way. Waiting until the hunters had left and the guards had posted themselves, she called Amu and made as if to join the females but once out of sight they turned to go in a different direction, walking into the savannah where she could practise her hunting skills.

Life became more interesting once she could continue teaching her child how to stalk and kill. Amu, imitating her mother while they looked for easy prey like hares and rodents, learnt how to interpret the slightest stirring of leaves, how to glide noiselessly moving like grass wafting with a breeze, and how to crawl slithering like a snake. Her mother taught her the crouching stance and forward creep in the camouflaging shadow of bushes, then the rush and run to chase the quarry, and the right moment to throw the hunting stick. Amu threw her missile first. At the same time Moogi's sped through the air with deadly accuracy, usually piercing the animal's throat. It was a game to Amu; for Moogi it was a pastime.

After killing their prey, sometimes even a small antelope, Moogi taught her daughter how to use the handaxe and scraper to skin the animal, how to cut it up, what to eat and what to leave. Entrails were thrown to the birds but main organs could be eaten there and then, though sparingly. After the kill there was danger that a predator would smell the blood and follow them, so that it was best to leave the carcass before returning hastily to the camp. Neither did Moogi want the fuzimo to know how adept she was at hunting.

One day while enjoying a feast of flesh after a kill, they had a fright when something rose from behind them and sprang forward with a triumphant shout. It was Feseta, a youngish female who sometimes still played with the children.

'Me follow,' she said proudly.

'You find feet?' Moogi asked and voicing admiration, 'you good-good.'

That was the beginning of their friendship and combined hunting excursions. Feseta learnt fast so that it became possible for one of the females to flush out the target flesh while the other took aim at it. Their activity was kept a secret, though Moogi could only hope that Feseta would not betray her, and she wondered what the other fuzimo thought when one of their group constantly went along with her. When she talked to the girl about the matter, Feseta answered, 'Me have no mother, she dead.'

'You have father?' Moogi asked.

'What is "father"?'

Moogi tried to explain about Joha having been father to Toma and Amu but Feseta failed to understand. This exchange led Moogi to reminisce about her lost males, the big strong good Toma and her own big strong good-good male Joha. They had taught her everything, she maintained and she took pride in showing Feseta how to make sharp-tipped hunting sticks, handaxes with cutting edges, or knobbly cudgels.

Amu, who had been shown all this often, avoided listening by wandering off to find something with which to play, and one day they heard her calling urgently, 'Come, come!' She had a hairy spider straddling her entire hand and was stroking it gently with the fingers of the other. It was obvious to Moogi that her child had been looking for birds' eggs and had found the huge spider sucking a fledgling dry.

'Put on tree,' commanded Moogi sternly.

Amu glanced at her with astonishment but obediently put her hand up to a branch. The petrified spider did not move, and Amu looking at her mother triumphantly, said, 'Ooki good, Ooki like me.'

'Put on tree,' repeated Moogi even more sternly. Amu gave the spider a helping push, and as if regaining its senses, it transferred to a twig that bent with its weight.

'Ooki like hand,' Amu concluded, regretting she had lost a playmate.

She had better tell her child more about dangerous spiders, Moogi decided, realising that all her previous teaching had not made Amu sufficiently cautious.

Hunting and the new friendship revived Moogi's spirits until the night that she was called out of her shelter by a female.

'Male want you.'

In the dark Moogi made out the second figure without knowing who it was. The moment she had feared was upon her, her mouth went dry, her throat constricted and she could not speak. The female melted into the dark, the male pulled her down beside the shelter on the side away from the camp and began to feel her all over. She thought of Amu, how happy she was playing with the children and that for her sake she must yield to this male. She bore his exploration in silence and when he put his ora in her, she remained unresponsive. Fortunately he was not one of the noisy copulating males but only breathed hard and let out a grunt of satisfaction on ejaculating. Shortly after, he rose and melted into the night as the female had done.

Moogi wiped herself with leaves, crawled into the shelter and lay awake for long, trying to think of what she could do.

Next day not one of the males in camp gave any sign of involvement. Who was the female who had brought the male to her? Which one was the male? Surely when the moon was shining, the males and females must recognise each other before mating? Why did the fuzimo choose a dark night to do that to her? The questions without answers once more ran round her thoughts like ants.

That night she lay awake waiting for the call from outside her shelter until weariness brought sleep. Nights passed and Moogi thought that perhaps she had been tried out and found wanting. Could she hope the males would leave her alone now? But though the fuzimo took no interest in where she went or what she did, they continued to make sporadic demands.

One night when Amu awoke and called and Moogi told her not to worry she would be back soon, the child came out. She bent over the fuzimo lying on top of her mother to see what was going on and asked, 'What you do?'

'He put ora in,' Moogi explained in a whispered aside, as the male was grunting and pushing without even having noticed the child.

'He go soon?' asked Amu sleepily.

'Yes,' Moogi assured her. 'Me come soon.'

Satisfied, Amu crawled back as the male ejaculated and shortly got up to go.

On her bed of grass again, Moogi thought long and hard of what she must do. She could not go on like that. The indifferent way the males used her made her so angry that she wanted to strangle them during sex.

Did the other females not mind? As they never talked to her, she could not ask. No, she would have to leave. The memory of the dangers, those wild dogs, filled her with a renewed terror that made her spend nights agonising about whether she should go or stay.

AMU SOLVES A PROBLEM

The Lady Archaeologist had two homes, one conventional with husband and a student son in a rambling house where bougainvillea blossoms invaded the veranda, and the vegetable garden was tended by one of Baratu's brothers, providing the family with all the greens they needed. The other was camp life under the old-fashioned ridge tent with its flysheet providing an air passage between the two areas of canvas, and a further elongation beyond the end pole for the "verandah" with camp-table and chairs. Here she ate the meals the cook conjured out of tins.

The fossil team had their shack sleeping quarters but preferred to sit out in the open in the evening round that congenial campfire, and the Lady Archaeologist when resident in camp sometimes joined the men. As she was getting old, her camp chair was a preference to sitting on the ground or on three-legged stools as they did.

On this particular evening the conversation revolved round marriage. The men of different tribal origins and from either town or rural locations, hotly discussed variations: the old way of paying brideprice in terms of head of cattle, Christian marriages before the altar, Asian marriages agreed between parents rather than by the young couple, and the latest 'modern' civil ceremony. Or, as one put it, just a man and woman living together. The mention of this form made the middle-aged fossil hunters shake their heads.

Then there was the additional factor of monogamy versus polygamy, the men arguing vehemently about the advantages of having several women to till the fields and many children to keep one in old age, as against the one wife whose labour might be insufficient to feed the family and whose fewer offspring provided no insurance.

The Lady Archaeologist who was mostly silent but did not want to be left out told them of another form. 'There is a kind of marriage where one woman is married to several husbands and we call it polyandry.'

'Po-ly-an-dry,' they chorused, 'must be bad.'

The very idea was outrageous. What about the children, would such few born to the one woman make the men happy? wondered one. The thought was enough to fuel further arguments. Perhaps one woman would cost the men less, perhaps the joint ownership of the children was also cheaper, suggested another. Oh yes, the shared cost of schooling would definitely be less per man, but what about sexual rights? Was this female going to be kept busy every night?

Baratu, to cool the hot discussion, turned to the Lady Archaeologist and asked about the possible composition of a hominin family. Would there have been a harem as among present day apes? What did palaeoanthropologists think?

'In a way, your arguments about the importance of children is what we think determined the form of the so-called family group. Mammal evolution points to everything in nature being geared to the production of offspring to keep a species going. So, as you say, apes gather a harem to spread their semen for lots of offspring, but as brains grew larger and the ape line evolved into hominins, there may have been a change in that arrangement.

'Both sexes will have had to contribute to their offsprings' welfare, finding vegetable foods and meat. Obviously two adults, father and mother, can do this better than just one, and several males and females forming a larger unit may have been even more advantageous. This may have led to a group of females living with a group of males, not in our sense of married couples but as a sort of cooperative for rearing children.'

'You mean anybody just going with anybody?' asked one of the men incredulously.

Baratu looked serious and shook his head. 'I can see this happening again,' he murmured.

— — — — — —

The fuzimo male or males, Moogi did not know how many, continued to visit her at night. Each started the same way, groping all over her body with small fingers like spiders let loose. The males took it for granted that she would relax her thighs so that they could push an ora into her without effort.

As the fuzimo were slim and short, their mounting was not uncomfortable but their unrestrained grunts at every thrust and possible final howl of satisfaction infuriated her increasingly. It was as though each male wanted the others to know how hard he was at work. The female's side of the copulation did not seem to count. To work off her fury and forget her troubles, she always took Amu and Feseta off to the hunting grounds next day as soon as the fuzimo turned to their tasks. What about Feseta whose breasts were beginning to fill? Moogi wondered. Was she already required at night? How long would it be before her own child would draw their attention, or would they continue to shy away from her? She felt trapped in a situation that she could not endure for much longer and yet as soon as she heard her name called, she felt obliged to get out of the shelter for the acts of the night.

Having observed the silent indifference of the fuzimo adults, it was all the more strange to hear the happy chatter of Amu's playmates. Older fuzimo girls like Feseta who helped in the camp chores also continued to be sociable, while older boys went off with the men to hunt but returned with exciting talk about the chase. So when did these younger fuzimo become morose adults? Moogi thought it happened once the young girls had a child that was left behind with a group of females while the rest foraged. As for the boys, they became increasingly quiet in the company of the men and finally as silent. Similarly, they probably copied their mating habits. Moogi was appalled to think that she might even have been called to the night-time orgy by one she had known as Amu's playmate.

While Amu and Feseta amused themselves playing at target practice at the hunting grounds or constructed toy animals with twigs and leaves and devised their fights with appropriate commentary, Moogi just sat and watched, brooding on her fate and wondering how to find shelter with a different horde. Looking around and into the distance there was nothing to prevent her from leaving any time. The opportunity was there and she decided to prepare a supply of hunting sticks and cudgels for both herself and Amu. On return to the campsite these were hidden under their bedding of grass.

Since the day Feseta had joined them on their outings, both she and Moogi took it in turn to act as lookout. Nevertheless it was Amu who alerted them to someone's approach.

'They come. They come!' she declared with absolute certainty one midday after gathering eggs which she clutched gently in each hand for delivery to her mother.

'Where?' Moogi asked immediately, looking near and far for the approach of fuzimo.

Amu looked away and became evasive. 'Oma hear, Oma good,' she addressed her tortoise, who had been allowed to forage for itself in their vicinity.

'What Oma hear?' Moogi questioned her.

'Oma hear they come.'

Feseta, listening to the statement, looked all round and then turned about herself to peer into the distance with eyes half-closed against the glare. 'No,' she declared. 'Amu play.'

Amu sat down and concentrated on heaping little mounds of sand into which she stuck whatever lay around her, while adding a commentary, 'This for Moogi, this for Feseta, this for Oma. Amu bad-bad, no thing for Amu.'

'Moogi! they come, they come,' she repeated suddenly and ducked down, waiting for her mother to do the same. 'Feseta, here,' she patted the ground next to her.

Moogi, remembering another occasion, complied and had to convince Feseta that somebody was coming if Amu said so. After a while Feseta, weary of the wait, rose to continue her foraging but found her hand pulled down.

'They come,' said Amu urgently. 'Lie.'

'Lie,' urged Moogi too.

Face to the ground they lay, while insects hummed around them and the sun's rays beat on their backs.

Gradually voices became audible. Moogi thought they were those of returning hunters. Amu's hand stole into her mother's, tense with apprehension. The slight crunch of feet on dry grass drew nearer as Moogi turned her head slowly to peer. She let out a shriek, jumped up and screamed unintelligibly, standing still only for a moment before taking off at speed towards the figures which had stopped in alarm.

There was an answering roar, 'Moogi!' and Moogi, reaching her goal, jumped into Joha's arms as she had done once before. Behind her Amu came running, shouting, laughing and being caught up in Toma's hug. Feseta stood at a distance, looking on bewildered.

It was some time before Joha and Moogi let go of each other and became capable of speech. Then it was Amu's turn to be swung up into her father's embrace, and Toma's turn to hug Moogi.

'You big, you good-good,' Joha admired his daughter, and Toma stroked Moogi's long hair lovingly.

By the time they had wandered towards Feseta it was Amu who took her hand, pulled her forward and said, 'Feseta.' Then as an afterthought she added, 'Fuzimo.'

The two males gazed at the young female and then turned to Moogi.

'This fuzimo?' asked Joha looking down at her with considerable unease.

Moogi was reminded of her first meeting with the fuzimo male who appeared to be frightened of Amu, little as she was at the time. Similarly her males exhibited fear of Feseta, hardly a formidable foe.

'This fuzimo good-good,' Moogi answered defensively, going to her side and placing an arm round her.

Joha emitted one of his grunts but Toma stared until Feseta's embarrassment made him look away. Equally Moogi could not take her eyes off the two males, so much taller and yet slimmer than she remembered either.

'You big,' she could not help exclaiming, measuring them up and down with an approving look and she skipped up to Joha, hugging him again and again.

'Moogi,' he kept muttering, 'Moogi.' More he could not say lost for words. He had Amu in his arms, hers round his neck, and he felt overwhelmed by the wonder of finding his females again when he had given them up for dead. At last finding expression he muttered to himself, 'He say go here, no go there, go here.'

'Who say?' enquired Moogi, and Toma looked at his father intently. But Joha turned away and would not answer.

They found a shady spot and sat in a circle. The females unloaded their pouches of foraged food; Joha and Toma contributed cuts of meat for a feast that calmed them into silence except for the sound of chewing.

'Water?' asked Joha after a while.

'At fuzimo camp.'

At that Joha became worried. 'Fuzimo camp? We go.' Overcome by the meeting, thought had been impossible until the mention of a fuzimo camp jolted him into action. The most urgent thing surely was to get away from them as fast and far as possible now that he had his family back.

But Toma looked round the circle and said, 'Moogi say.'

The shock of seeing her males alive resulted in a surge of overwhelming happiness that had swamped Moogi's thoughts as well. Toma's remark brought her back to the prevailing situation. Should they all go to the fuzimo camp?

What for? she asked herself. If the fuzimo shied away from Amu, how would they react to Joha and Toma who were so much taller and surely would look menacing to the little men? What was to stop her and Amu, now sitting contentedly on her father's lap, from going with them, away from the camp, away from the fuzimo she so desired never to see again. But there was Feseta. If they did not return her would the fuzimo not come after them with their skill of tracking and their superior number that could easily overcome them.

Joha had intercepted the long thoughtful look Moogi had given the female. How could they get rid of Feseta? He looked at his cudgel. One blow and the problem would be solved. But the thought troubled him. The likeness of Feseta with Moogi, the same black long hair, light skin and slim body was astonishing. He knew killing her was impossible and so what should they do?

All through the meal Toma had hardly been able to tear his glance from the young female's breasts that confused his mind even more than the extraordinary event. He tried to look away and waited for Moogi to announce a decision.

'Feseta you go camp,' Moogi suddenly commanded.

'Me no go camp,' she declared looking defiantly at the family. 'Me have no mother, Moogi mother for me.'

Moogi and Joha exchanged worried glances, realising she could not be forced to return.

During another silence, this time of indecision, Amu glanced from one to the other of the adults. She had been listening and was aware of the waves of uncertainty in their minds but why, when the course of action was so clear to her. She leaned over to Moogi and taking her hand, put it in Joha's. Then she rose, pulled Feseta to her feet, led her to Toma who had jumped up too, and placed one of her hands in Toma's.

'We go,' she said with finality and began looking for Oma.

Feseta held tightly on to Toma's hand, looking up at him imploringly. He met her glance, stole another look at her breasts, put an arm round her and said, 'Me take Feseta.'

The tension broken, Joha gave his son a loving tap on the shoulder and Moogi took the female's other hand to squeeze it.

Meanwhile Amu had loaded Oma into a food bag, and having passed it to her mother was beginning to walk away followed by the rest making a straggling line.

A while later Joha stood still to listen to his inner voice. He hurried to the front and took his family off in a different direction. Silently, fearful of meeting some of the camp fuzimo, the group trotted after Joha. Under a sun moving imperceptibly from one side of the horizon to the other, they felt increasingly safe when their savannah world remained empty.

After the event of reunion Joha found a renewed purpose in marching to his unknown destination. The chance meeting, as he believed, the amazing way his female and child had suddenly run towards him when he thought them long dead, filled his mind with wonder and great satisfaction. The terrible longing for his family ceased, replaced instead by happiness and the belief that his voice's instructions must be good-good.

Being together again made him feel they were now less vulnerable from danger, and the willingness of Feseta to be Toma's female removed the burden of finding him one. During their marches the young couple often lingered behind and finally disappeared from view. At first this troubled Joha who could not forget how Toma had once walked out of their lives, but somewhere further along the trail the two would join them again hand in hand and looking happy. Moogi guessed what was going on.

'Toma, Feseta ...' and she made a gesture, winding one finger round another on the opposite hand.

Joha after looking somewhat startled grunted, 'Good-good.'

For their nightly shelter, each couple by unspoken consent chose a spot not too near each other, and once Amu had gone to sleep Joha caressed his female to his heart's content, shown by his deep grunts and final exhaled sighs of satisfaction.

How Moogi had longed to hear these. All in place of the fuzimo final howls during her ordeal, not to forget their groping spider fingers.

Joha's joyful hugs at dawn contrasted markedly with the bland faces of those other males, so that during the day's journey Moogi frequently broke into song from sheer happiness.

SNAKES?

Latterly the search for hominin remains had been disappointing, therefore the men during their campfire discussions agreed to try a sweep for fossils by walking in a line, fanning out a few metres apart.

Baratu suggested they should spend as long as it took to walk along all the bays and promontories marked on the geologists' map, until they had been round at least their side of the 'lake' area.

This took considerable time, during which they made several surface finds of pieces belonging to animal fossils. The locations were not only noted on the map but also indicated by stone cairns for later excavation.

It was while walking in company with the others that Baratu felt his buzz. Nothing noteworthy showed on the land surface, so he pretended seeing an object of interest and bent down to place some stones on the spot in the shape of his initials.

The subsequent digs kept the camp going for weeks. the test trench under Baratu's cairn, however, yielded nothing.

He had heard a buzz, the whispering voices, something must be there. So he returned to do something much frowned upon, namely digging on his own. He opened up the trench again and began to trowel round the previously dug hole. Carefully he loosened a few small clods at a time, removing the soil with a brush to make sure he would see a fossil before digging into it. After several hours of painstakingly removing layer upon layer, determined to find what the buzz had promised, he was not surprised when a shiny brown surface appeared under the bristles. Delicate removal of earth with a dental pick revealed curvature, until he thought it possible that it might be a fossil skull. He covered it with earth and returned to camp to call up the Lady Archaeologist.

'Hello, it's Baratu here. I have found something that looks like part of a fossil skull.'

News like that always brought her as soon as she could arrange an early supply plane. The team accompanied her to their various successful digs which she viewed enthusiastically, fully understanding why Baratu said nothing until next day when he led her to his. One glance at the shiny surface of the fossil and she became visibly excited.

'We'll do the usual survey tomorrow and take it from there. Unless we're mistaken this is not just a fragment.'

It turned out to be the find of his career: almost a complete skull and jaw and most of the fossilised skeleton of a hominin. The excitement in the camp reached fever pitch, though little was said. The whole crew sat at the worktable, cleaning, sorting, and joining fragments. They had suggested sending the finds to the Museum on the next plane but the Lady Archaeologist reminded them that there might be some pieces missing, and that they still had the chance of digging further to find them. A preliminary assembling was essential.

After hours of concentrated work taking two days, the skeleton almost complete lay on the worktable ready for packing and transportation, while the team sat back to admire their masterpiece.

'Looking at the pelvis I believe it is a female,' said the Lady Archaeologist. 'Most fortunate for our study of birthing.'

'Why is giving birth important?' asked one of the men. 'After all, it happens all the time, then and now.'

'You're right, of course,' answered the Lady, 'but I'm sure you have noticed how easily animals give birth and how difficult it can be for human females. The difficulty must have started with bipedalism that requires the legs to be close together, otherwise we would waddle. This in turn causes the pelvis opening to be smaller.'

The men all turned towards her, their attention captured.

'By contrast, evolution shows heads got bigger as brains developed,' the Lady continued, 'and a time must have come when females began to have difficulty with birth. Head bigger, pelvis opening smaller – you get the picture.'

'Head bigger, pelvis opening smaller,' repeated one man as if learning by rote.

'That's right!' confirmed the Lady. 'And it's worth mentioning again that as a result the infant is born before it is ready for the world. In other words, nature lets the head out before it could become trapped in the womb.'

'Not ready for the world. Wait until I tell my wife when I go home,' remarked the same man.

'Yes, well, although all these changes took a very long time,' continued the Lady, 'it would be nice to know when they became critical in human evolution. If we were to find many pelvises, there might be some answers.'

Baratu was fascinated by the revealed facts. His wife, being a midwife, would surely want to know when hominins started to have birthing difficulties so that they needed helping hands. He asked the Lady Archaeologist about it.

'That is another question currently being discussed,' she said. 'Apes give birth easily because the child's head and the configuration of the pelvis are made for one another. As I said, evolution in creating the big head has caused a problem these more intelligent hominins had to solve and probably their females did begin to help each other. But 'when' is the question palaeontologists are asking, as you are.'

– – – – – –

Their reunion made Joha aware of his family as never before. Every time he glanced at Toma it was with satisfaction at his height, the long legs, the body hair that grew on him now he was older, his male organs which hung more prominently, and his massive shoulders and arms indicating great strength. It was almost impossible to remember the skeletal form he had carried for so long.

Amu's strong body, her quick understanding and child's playfulness, were his joy.

He eyed Feseta critically but with approval. The breasts were becoming fuller, her slim child's stature was rounding into firm buttocks and wider hips and of course her resemblance to Moogi in being lighter in skin colour and similarly longhaired endeared her to him.

Moogi had changed from being his young female to being an adult and smelling like one. It increased his desire for her and excited his ora. In addition her self-possessed attitude made her a real mate. He liked seeing her reaching up to pluck fruit, breasts pointing out and upwards, or bending down when he would look at her rounded buttocks with pleasure, and lately he had realised her smooth front had begun to round in a slight hump. Presently he could no longer contain himself and putting his big hand on it and almost grinning, he announced, 'Child in here.'

Moogi startled, looked down and felt herself and began to laugh, remembering the previous occasion when Joha had said the same. She marvelled at the way he could spark off a child in her as soon as they were together again. What a desirable male, and she wondered whether Toma would be as good at making a child in Feseta whose tummy had not yet distended.

Amu came up and put her hand where her father's had been. 'Child?' she asked wide-eyed.

Moogi, convinced Joha was right, told her a tiny child would come out and Amu would then be able to play with its little feet and hands.

'It come?'

'No,' Moogi explained, 'not now,' and in her mind wondered when she could tell Amu that it was coming.

During these exchanges Toma and Feseta had looked and listened with interest and they too came up to feel Moogi's stomach. Joha was surprised that Toma did not remember last time Moogi had grown a front hump. For her part, Moogi thought of the fuzimo females who had those big tummies and appeared one day with a child, without anybody knowing where the birth had taken place.

On their continuing safari Joha reduced his jogging pace, to her relief, though it mattered little to Toma and Feseta who adhered to their habit of disappearing for a part of each day, mostly returning with a contribution of flesh. They always maintained it was easy to read Joha's huge footprint. Moogi's suspicion about their activities was confirmed by the silence of their night shelter in comparison with hers, in which Joha was often very demonstrative so that he had to be reminded of her increasing girth.

Since the family reunion there was a burning question in Moogi's mind. How had the males found each other? But whenever she broached the subject, Joha answered evasively and Toma said he did not understand her, he and his father had always been together. They had stayed with an old fuzimo and a young child in a cave. They had eaten good flesh and eventually had gone on their way. When Joha showed her the use of animal horns from which to drink and taught her to throw the bolas pebbles to ensnare a prey's feet, she realised they had been with a 'good' male. In return Joha was pleased that their lost gourds had been replaced while Moogi was staying with her band of fuzimo. Even Amu had a small one tied to a thong and slung from across one shoulder.

On their daily marches now Moogi trudged a little way behind the others, too tired to notice her surroundings. Joha was not worried about her lack of energy: that tummy was huge and he could not help feeling it from time to time, wondering when his new child would emerge.

One day when Moogi slowly caught up with them, they were pointing excitedly at a part of the sky in the distance that had gone dark. Joha remembered the stampede and while they were still watching, his fears were confirmed as a long line of animals became visible running towards them.

'We go!' he shouted, swinging Amu onto his back and took off towards a slight rise, his mind in shocked disbelief that the previous experience was about to be repeated. Toma and Feseta had meanwhile joined up with them and seeing Moogi could not run took an arm on each side and propelled her along as fast as she could move up to higher ground.

The dark sky turned into billowing clouds behind the animals that by now had veered away from the rise and were thundering past below them. The clouds swirled, black, grey and white, ever nearer, and in them were snakes leaping this way and that, coiling, writhing and slithering. Coloured

red, orange and black, they leaped high and low, threw themselves sideways or returned to slide along the ground in flickers of light. Some caught up with the rearmost runners who fell over dead, or chased other animals white-eyed with terror, bellowing and bleating and trying to get away by leaping wildly over rocks and bushes.

To Joha and Moogi this all looked like the stampede they had witnessed, antelopes, leopards and cheetahs all running side by side, ahead of the heavier grazers.

The family stood paralysed with fear, listening to the hissing and crackling of the snakes from which hot air wafted up like hot breath. A terrible stench reached them together with showers of black particles in a grey cloud which enveloped everything and made them cough and stung their eyes.

Joha heard his inner voice shouting, 'Go!' and boomed it out to the others. Through chinks in the blinding swirl he could see a line of vegetation in the distance and began running downhill towards it, still carrying Amu on his back.

Moogi gathered all her strength and stumbled on, stopped from falling by her supporters, until at last they reached the river where they drank to stop their coughing. Relief was short-lived because on lifting their heads there was the noise of the approaching snakes, now a roaring sound that stupefied their senses. Bushes and reeds erupted with the creatures, again crackling and hissing, and leaping in and out of the vegetation. They wound round tree trunks, ever upwards, and writhed in the branches that broke off with a crack like lightning. More hot particles rained down, acrid clouds wafted across the water causing renewed coughing and spluttering. Terror-stricken the family waded across, slid and slithered in their effort to scramble up the further bank, and smashing through vegetation with their sticks ran after Joha who kept shouting, 'Go! Go!'

Panting and exhausted they had to stop after a while to regain their breath. Amu, cuddled in her father's arms, fell asleep.

Moogi looking thoughtful and still gulping air remarked, 'This hot…buhu…stink.'

Toma agreed, he too had noticed the 'hot' killing the buhu and making it smell dreadfully. Where had this 'hot' come from, was it a predator moving faster than most animals? It had even tried to attack them.

Once Moogi had regained her breath, Joha urged them to move on for safety, and although the sun was low they continued walking until dark. Erecting two flimsy shelters the best they could, they saw in the far distance a line of bright red flickering light.

'The 'hot' sleeping there,' Toma pointed out. 'We good here.'

Joha had his bad nights after their experience. Flood-water piled up in a wave about to crash down on him, or he saw a mountain spewing streams of blood into the sky with huge blobs raining down them, or he was standing on the edge of a wall of earth and felt himself falling, falling, and being buried alive. His legs moved as if in a spasm, arms flailed, he wanted to scream and emitted only guttural exclamations and at times clutched Moogi so tightly that she woke in a fright. Such interrupted sleep made him tired next day, irritable, and he sat apart from the others, only Amu being able to jolly him back into a semblance of his former self.

Amu and her father were marching ahead slowly, when Moogi, as usual bringing up the rear, sank to her knees with a cry of pain. Joha rushed to her but she warded him off with her hands, leaned back on her elbows, spread her legs and passed water. She panted, let out little shrieks, grunted and whimpered, unlike any sound he had ever heard coming from her.

Amu sat by her bewildered and anxious, looking from one parent to the other. Joha guessing what was about to happen, began calling Toma by means of several bellows that reverberated round the rocky outcrop where Moogi had stopped.

Although there was no answer the couple came running full tilt from between trees and bushes a little while later weapons to hand, and stopped short before Moogi who by now was straining to bear down and labouring with even faster pants. Feseta at once knelt down to support her back and Toma offered a sympathetic hand that Moogi pulled on in her exertion. Joha sat to one side looking helpless.

The sun's rays beat down hot but Moogi was so preoccupied that she could not be persuaded to move into the shadow of bushes. Although she pushed with all her might, panted and pushed again, at times howling like an animal, nothing appeared and she became so exhausted that she went limp, and with eyes shut looked almost dead.

Fear gripped Feseta. She had overheard women talking at her camp about their births and how females died who could not push their child out. Was that what was happening to Moogi? She made Toma exchange places with her, knelt between Moogi's legs, stroked her thighs gently to keep her awake and said authoritatively, 'Push!'

It was as if Moogi woke up from sleep and took several seconds to orientate.

'Push!' Feseta commanded and Moogi began to push again with renewed vigour, grunting and screaming, sometimes drumming her feet on the ground in agony, until Feseta held her down by the thighs, shouting encouragement at the same time. At last the head crowned. Feseta gave a hoot of triumph, cupped one hand round the child's head and eased it out while pushing back the taut skin round it with the fingers of her other hand. Head born, the shoulders, arms and legs began to slide out gradually until the child lay in the sandy soil, besmeared with blood, still and dead-looking. For a moment everyone stared in horror. Then Feseta took it by the legs, held it up, shook it and slapped it gently on the back, remembering what she had heard the women say.

It gave a small cry, coughed, and cried more lustily. Feseta suddenly aware of what she was doing, handed it to Moogi who cradled the wet, bloody boy-child in her arms and regarded it with astonishment. Black hair clung damp to the strangely shaped, rather big head, but when it opened its eyes to squint at her, she hugged it to her breasts and put her cheek next to the tiny one.

Feseta was asked to pass her a gourd of water so that she could wash the child. Still Joha sat motionless, deeply engrossed in staring at what looked almost like a replica of Moogi or Feseta, a slim, black-haired and light-skinned child but with a big head.

Amu's eyes had grown ever bigger during these proceedings. She had moved forward to see what was happening between her mother's legs and exclaimed with delight when the head came through and eventually the face showed.

After a while during which there was silent relief while Moogi rested and cuddled her child, she expelled the afterbirth, and remembering previous experience cut the cord from her child's navel with a handaxe.

Toma placed large leaves around the afterbirth and cord and threw it all into a bush.

It was only then that Moogi handed Joha the child. He took it gently in his big hands, held it up to his face and pronounced, 'Badili – child for me.'

The others were taken aback for a moment.

'Badili?'

'Badili, child before Toma,' Joha explained.

Moogi momentarily astonished was far too happy to ask further questions. 'Badili good-good,' she agreed and after she had cleaned herself they settled to a much-needed meal from their food pouches.

Toma suggested they call a halt for the day. Together with Feseta and Amu, he fetched twigs and grass for the shelters and bedding, choosing the softest leaves for Badili's nest.

Joha just sat holding his son, murmuring, 'Badili, Badili,' until Moogi wanted to give him the breast. The child took the offered nipple while Amu closely inspected what was going on. She found Oma and held it up so the tortoise could see Badili in action.

'Look!' she said, 'he get water from Moogi.'

That night Joha had his worst nightmare. Moogi was on the ground writhing with pain. She contorted herself into strange shapes, first resembling a choking hyena, then a coiled snake, and suddenly she looked like a gnarled club, terribly ugly and animal-like. He began to convulse with fear, his body shuddered, his arms and legs moved as if hitting and kicking something to the accompaniment of snarling in his sleep.

When his arm landed on Moogi she awoke and sensing something was wrong patted him gently. Startled he reared up, hitting his head on the shelter roof, which woke him fully. He was disorientated and upset and only when she found his hand in the dark to place on Badili for reassurance did he calm sufficiently to lie down again and then slept past sunrise.

BADILI PROVES A POINT

The campfire was located some distance from the Lady Archaeologist's tent so that its smoke would not be blown into her entrance. On nights when the fossil team were not busy at their worktable dealing with sorting and cataloguing, the voices and laughter coming from the direction of the fire were a welcome sound in a somewhat lonely world around her, although she could rely on Baratu's visit early in the evening for a discussion of next day's work.

This time when he appeared it was with uncharacteristic hurry. 'Lady, could you come? Some of the men are getting angry over a silly argument.'

Surprised and somewhat dismayed, the Lady Archaeologist immediately took the torch and hurried to the fireside where two of the men were conversing in raised voices. Baratu had brought her camp chair, into which she let herself down in a calm off-duty manner.

The two protagonists hardly noticed her as their talk reached shouting pitch.

Baratu intervened. 'I have brought the Lady to listen to each of you in turn and she will settle the matter.'

Without an inkling of what it was about, she trusted Baratu wasn't landing her in an impossible situation and waited to hear the subject of the uproar.

'In Africa we dig up fossils of hominins,' said one of the angry men, 'and people like us working in Asia and Europe are digging them up as well. So there must have been animals there that evolved into man-like creatures.'

'I've already told you!' said the other man. 'We hear all the time that it's here in Africa that we dig up the earliest fossils of creatures which then evolved into men. It was after that they spread all over the world.'

'Always the same story!' exclaimed another one of the team almost under his breath. Then continuing more audibly, 'Have you never heard that God made the world in six days, fish, birds, animals, man and woman? When people call them man and woman they mean male and female of the ape-hominins line. Then they started evolving – and spread all over the world. All creatures are different to what they were when God first made them.'

Baratu put up his hand. 'Lady, it's your turn.'

'You have been very inventive with all your ideas about the origin of hominins. Each of you has been right in some way.'

Baratu understood she was trying to pour water on hot embers without offering her own explanation. 'What do the scientists think?' he asked.

'Well, instead of enumerating all their arguments about the origin of mankind, I'll tell you of an idea you haven't mentioned and which might be more interesting to discuss. It's called the Aquatic Ape Theory and people who believe in it argue like this: we are like chimpanzees and gorillas which prefer areas with trees and yet we don't, and are very different in other aspects. All right, so we're supposed to have moved from forest to grassland and adapted to living in the savannah but whether we lived among trees or in grasslands, it's the way our bodies are built that is difficult to explain unless we once lived partly in water.'

'Water?' they chorused incredulously. 'Humans being like fish?'

'No, not like fish,' said the Lady. 'Just hear me out. You see, our nakedness, the white fat we are born with under our skin, and our bipedalism are ideal for swamp living. Proboscis monkeys in Borneo and Bonobos in West Africa walk upright quite easily and partly live in swamps.

'There are also other features of our body: we have conscious control of our breathing only found in aquatic animals like seals and dolphins, and diving birds like penguins. Then there is the peculiarity of our larynx that descends in the throat a few months after the baby is born so we can take a big gulp of air when we dive, like sea lion and dugong. And now you can have a laugh when I tell you that the walrus, seal and sea otter can weep from their eyes when excited or frustrated.

'More seriously, scientists maintain that to grow a bigger brain you need something called Omega-3 fatty acids, and you get plenty of it in seafoods and less in nourishment grown on land.'

By this time the men were listening with disbelief in their expressions. 'Sea apes, living in water,' exclaimed one. 'Oh no!'

'Nothing but big frogs!' muttered another and made them laugh.

‒ ‒ ‒ ‒ ‒ ‒

Badili was as healthy as his first lusty cry. Being slim and long-limbed he sat up long before Amu had done as a baby and even crawled much earlier, so that they quickly became playmates. She selected the roundest pebbles to roll towards him, until Moogi found some in his mouth and had to select the safer size herself. Amu sat him on her hip for a few steps, proudly imitating her father who carried him for most of the time. She helped to wash him in river water under the watchful eye of Moogi or Joha and when he started eating solids, fed him juicy fruits and the 'aaaaaa' worms she favoured. The adults had to be careful that she was not giving him a tarantula or centipede in her enthusiasm. At first Amu had missed her fuzimo friends; Badili was their substitute. Oma was still her playmate when her half-brother was asleep but when she acted the hopping of frogs or swinging gait of giant lizards on the run, the tortoise showed no sign of being amused where Badili smiled and giggled responsively. Moogi's children gurgled a laugh from early babyhood, in contrast to Joha and Toma who once had to learn from her how to express mirth.

Moogi, looking at their water gourds dangling by thongs, wondered how she could make a sling for carrying Badili. Whenever Joha skinned flesh she asked for strips from the hide but when she made them into a net-like seat carried on her back with ties to reach over her shoulders, it was so hard and rough when dry that it hurt the child's bottom. Joha did not want it, declaring he would rather carry Badili however much it slowed him down.

Long leaves, woven to form a carrier of sorts with ties to reach over Moogi's shoulders, tore when dry until eventually she hit on the idea of cutting a piece of skin with her handaxe to make a seat. Unfortunately it soon began to stink. Joha scraped another piece down to the bare hide. Cut to the right size and dried until stiff, it proved successful for the short periods he allowed her to carry the child. A pad of soft grass made a good cushion and could be renewed when soiled. Thongs threaded through holes on each side crossed between her breasts and returned over her shoulders. A few bits of thong tied horizontally between the straps stopped Badili from falling out backwards or sideways.

The family's rest stops and camps were now filled with the noise of children's cries and laughter, very different from the days when Joha and his two older ones had stopped exhausted to erect a shelter. But as before, at dawn the family members crawled out of their shelters, picked up their goods and after Joha said, 'We go,' followed in his indicated direction. Toma often tried to stop his father by pointing out that they were about to leave a source of water, could they not stay a while at such a favourable camping site? Joha, deaf to all this, strode on and Toma and Feseta had to make their own decision about remaining behind or marching with him, which they had done so far.

Thorn tree and thorn bush savannah and the occasional islands of hills overgrown with leafy forests gave way to sandy soil and tall fronded trees. The herds of the plains were no longer in sight and the family tried eating vegetation new to them. Joha wondered whether his inner voice was leading them astray, especially when Toma and Feseta argued about returning to the places where there was plenty of flesh to be hunted.

Their journey took on a new interest when they found big fruits scattered on the ground below the tall trees. The inner nutshell could be cracked with a stone, allowing the travellers to drink the juice and eat the white flesh within. A few dawns later the family trudged through fine sand that slid between the toes, the trees thinned out, suddenly there before them was a huge expanse of water that made them gasp with astonishment.

The children ran forward to take a drink. Toma who had taken off after them gave a roar, 'Iiiiiiiiih!' and spat it out, followed by the others doing the same. Amu laughed, got Oma out of the pouch and introduced the tortoise to the sea that made it retract the head immediately until she took it away from the shore to a grassy patch.

The family stared at the unending water and the gently lapping waves with wonder. Seeing no crocodiles or hippos in sight Moogi walked into the warm ocean, jumped over the small incoming waves, shouted with delight and began swimming about. Amu and especially Badili followed without fear, finding their own way of dog paddling.

A shout from Toma on the beach, 'Where Badili?' alerted Moogi.

They all looked around but he was nowhere to be seen. Moogi, Feseta and Toma waded into deeper water, frantically sloshing around to find him. Joha shouted his name from the shore and ran up and down helpless to do anything in his fear of water, thereby missing Amu's piping voice telling them that Badili's head was bobbing up and down a little way further out between the waves. He was paddling contentedly, sometimes just below the water's surface and then above to take in air. Moogi who was an excellent swimmer at last caught sight of him and immediately set off to bring him back. The others were filled with astonishment that the toddler could swim like Moogi.

Joha took him into his generous embrace and did not want to let go, but Badili struggled and cried until allowed to toddle back to the sea where he could swim and dive, this time under the watchful eye of the females. The males sat on the beach until the hot sand burnt their bottoms and made them start to forage food, shellfish, crabs and seaweed, all new to taste.

Later that day they found a stream emptying into the sea. Drinking fresh water and having filled their stomachs with unaccustomed seafoods, the lulling sound of the waves and the soft cooler sand in the shade of the palms all contributed to sending them fast asleep. On waking and to their astonishment the ocean had retreated, leaving a wide stretch of wet ground across which it was possible to walk and meet the water lazily lapping round their feet. Joha despite his fear of the sea felt his sore toes soothed in the warm salt liquid.

By now his feet were infested with jiggers he was unwilling to dig out each dawn or dusk, which neglect had caused the flesh round his toenails to fester. Moogi rubbed chewed earth into them but they had not improved

He limped along determined to follow his voice and to carry his son as often as possible. Toma offered help, Moogi might point at the empty sling seat, Joha in his stubbornness only agreed to hand Badili over when his feet became too painful.

The journey now followed the shore. Amu and Badili had to be dragged away from their play of digging holes in the wet sand so that they could watch the water seeping in, and Feseta and Toma often lingered by rock pools, fascinated by crabs and jellyfish, until they had to run to catch up. The sun always sank swiftly behind the palms while shelters were being erected high up on the beach on soft dry sand. The children went to sleep at once, Amu on the warm sand, Badili in a nest of grass. The pain in Joha's feet reduced by walking at the edge of the saltwater made him feel so much better that he turned to Moogi for his old ways of arousing her. She in turn responded, hungry for sex.

At dawn he crawled from the shelter feeling satisfied that he was a large male in charge of a good-sized family. 'We go,' he shouted to everybody, hauling Badili from his nest and swinging him up onto his shoulders. The rest had a hard time snatching at their belongings to follow. Moogi and Amu hurried to keep pace, the other two as usual went their own way, meeting the family again further on.

After midday when Badili had done his stint of walking and Joha and Moogi had done theirs of carrying him, they were all ready to rest from the intense heat. Oma was let out of the food bag and the children looked for choice blades of grass to feed it.

One day Amu stopped in the middle of play, looked at the adults and said, 'They come!' She clutched her father anxiously, so that he got up with a searching glance in all directions.

'You see Toma?'

'No.'

'You see Feseta?'

Amu looked away and did not answer. Moogi also surveyed the immediate area but there was no sign of the others.

'They come!' Amu said again, hurriedly stuffing Oma back in his pouch. Moogi looked troubled. 'She know,' she told Joha.

Before they had time to consider the matter, a fuzimo stepped out from a group of trees some way off, shouting, and brandished his hunting stick. For a moment it looked as though he might be hunting flesh and was possibly unaware of them. The family, frightened by his sudden appearance, waited breathlessly for his next move. The fuzimo looked in their direction, shouted louder and raised his hunting stick as if to throw it at them despite the distance. It posed a challenge which Joha met with a roar. He grabbed his hunting sticks and ran towards him. The fuzimo shouted even louder but then ducked behind the trees, while Joha bellowing by way of response followed and disappeared as well.

Moogi who had called a warning, 'No!' which went unheeded, stood up grasping one of her hunting sticks, ready to face two fuzimo who had broken cover and came racing towards the little group. They stopped short when her stick landed at their feet. Amu beside her aimed her little one as well. They registered amusement and eyeing Moogi warily, advanced, walking towards mother and children, swinging their cudgels. It was obvious that the fuzimo band had played a trick by luring Joha away, leaving his family unprotected.

The two burly males of a darker, hairier and wilder-looking type than the ones Moogi had known, kept moving towards the family without hurry but twirling their weapons almost carelessly, leaving her in no doubt that they meant capture or possibly might kill her and take the children. Of Joha there was no sign. Badili, terrified, had his little arms round Amu who stood defiant and unafraid.

It was a desperate situation, one adult against two, and the expression on the males' faces as they came nearer, step by step, had already changed to one of triumph.

Moogi reached for her handaxe. Positioning herself sideways but keeping them in view, she swung an arm back and sent the missile flying in an arc edge on. It cut through the air at the height of the males' legs. There was a dreadful 'crack!' The nearest fuzimo screamed, his legs buckled and he fell moaning and holding his limb. The second fuzimo stopped in his tracks, glanced at the broken leg, turned and streaked back towards the palm grove.

From another direction, Toma and behind him Feseta, came running having heard the shouts, and arrived in time to see Moogi's defensive throw. Toma swung his cudgel, there was another cracking sound, he had split the Fuzimo's head but then like his father he too took off, pursuing the second attacker.

Moogi retrieved her handaxe from near the dead fuzimo, steadying herself ready to defend her family. Feseta raised her hunting stick as well and Amu had pebbles in her hand for missiles, so that when no fuzimo returned she aimed them at the dead body for practice.

The females remained standing for a long time prepared for battle, hoping for an early return of their males. Eventually Toma turned up saying he had lost the trail of the escaping fuzimo although at first it had been very visible in the sand and had crossed with that of others, Joha's as well.

They waited patiently for him, becoming increasingly concerned over his absence. Toma was in two minds and therefore did not know what to do. When he asked Moogi, she told him to stay and defend the family. Joha would have to look after himself which she was sure he could do.

The sun went its way, the day passed by. Amu practised her aim with pebbles and told Oma about the threatening fuzimo. Toma kept getting up to peer into the distance and climbed to the crown of a tree to have a better view. Moogi sat exhausted by the ordeal but vigilant, while Feseta looked after Badili.

Their anxiety increased when they considered what to do with the dead fuzimo over whom the flies were beginning to buzz. Surely his companions would come to fetch the body, and even if not, the vultures and hyenas were sure to arrive followed by bigger predators, even though they had not seen any for days.

Where was Joha, hurrying back or possibly lying somewhere wounded, unable to return to them? No, they had better not look for him among the tall trees for fear of walking into a fuzimo ambush. When the vultures arrived, tearing at the body, Moogi made a decision.

'We go,' she said. 'Joha see feet.'

They picked up their pouches and weapons and left to walk in the direction taken before the event. Having put distance between themselves and the body, Moogi called another halt as evening approached, so that they could prepare for the night's rest.

At dawn, there was Joha asleep between the shelters. In fact he did not stir despite their astonished exclamations. Waiting for him to wake, they attended to their tool kits: re-sharpening hunting sticks with the prepared edge of a handaxe, and tightening the thongs of their bolas slings. Amu tried to teach Badili how to build a toy shelter with twigs and tufts of grass; Moogi dug up tubers for a meal and the young couple eventually went off hand in hand saying they would not be far in case of trouble.

When Joha awoke he did so with a start, feeling for his hunting stick. 'Stick?' he asked perplexed. 'Stick for me.'

Amu came to help him search.

'Iiiih!' he exclaimed suddenly. 'Stick in fuzimo.' His memory of the previous day's events flooded back. After the challenge by the fuzimo he had trailed him but as the male was like an animal knowing its boltholes, it took Joha a long time to keep flushing him out. Finally he stayed visible and challenged Joha again.

'Me throw stick down, fight fuzimo with hands,' he told them with satisfaction. 'Me kill him!' showing how he strangled the male. 'Me put hunting stick in flesh,' he concluded, looking at Moogi for approval.

On listening to all this intently, Amu went to find Oma on which she tried to demonstrate what she had heard. Fortunately for the tortoise it was able to retract its neck.

Moogi kept murmuring, 'Good-good!' despite remembering in what peril he had left her and the children and considering he had lost all his weapons so that they spent the next few dawns waiting for him to make himself a new set.

When the young couple returned to be told of his adventure, Toma drew his father aside for harsh words. 'You leave Moogi, Amu, Badili for danger. Fuzimo come to kill.' Then he demonstrated Moogi's skilful throw of the handaxe, something none of them had ever tried.

Joha all remorseful but unable to find words to express it, hugged her and that night to show his appreciation put his ora in her hands.

The family resumed their marches without any further fuzimo trouble though always on the lookout for the enemy. The voice gave Joha no peace. He often looked at Amu to see whether she heard it too.

After all had they not recently experienced her ability to hear without seeing anyone? There was also Moogi's account of how Amu had heard the approaching footsteps of the fuzimo from her camp, and had known of Joha and Toma's coming before Moogi and Feseta could see them.

OUT OF AFRICA

Having explained the Aquatic Ape Theory of hominine evolution to her fossil team on the previous night, the Lady Archaeologist woke with a bad conscience that she had sidetracked the discussion, rather like the naughty schoolgirl of her youth who loved to involve her teacher in topics outside the curriculum. She resolved to make amends that night by returning to the main subject.

When Baratu turned up in the evening to discuss next day's work, she asked him to open a box of beer cans she had stowed away for a treat, and to distribute them among the team round the campfire. Would he please carry her chair there as she was going to join them.

Once everybody held a can and she had her bottle of soda water, the conversation flowed until she interrupted it with her apology.

'Yesterday evening I was asked to judge which of your ideas about the spread of hominins was the right one. As this is a contentious subject scientists like arguing about, I avoided it by introducing the Aquatic Ape Theory.

'I suppose that was an unfair evasion. So today I will deal with the ideas expressed yesterday and mention a theory which best fits the fossil finds of Africa and elsewhere.

'It seems that the hominin line arose in Africa about six million years ago and evolved through many intermediary forms. Evolution continued until they became recognisably us.

'These early humans must have migrated because subsequently they are found in other parts of the world. Not that they moved in one safari but possibly many, and where did they go? Well, if you look at the map, the easiest places to cross from Africa to Asia and to Europe is where the land masses almost join in the areas of the Red Sea and North Africa.'

There was a pause while more cans were distributed and the men discussed that it was unlikely that any hominin could have swum across the seas unless it had been an aquatic creature.

'Do you mean these migrating hominins were these aquatic ones you told us about, or did they have canoes by that time?' asked one of the team.

'No. There is another idea of how they got across: earth movement, volcanoes and severe climatic conditions are always changing land formation. So perhaps similarly these factors may have caused seas or channels in these areas to become narrower and sandbanks to appear. Surely animals and humans of one sort or another saw their opportunity to find more places for foraging food and therefore swam across or walked over land bridges from Africa to what is now Arabia and so to Asia and Europe.'

'What do you call this idea?' another man asked.

'It's known as the Out of Africa Theory.'

'Do you believe this one?'

'Yes. Our DNA research confirms that we are all one people with our ancestry in Africa.'

The men sat in silence, remembering their own theories and arguments. The Lady Archaeologist stared into the fire with a faraway look.

'But,' she continued suddenly, 'we had better remember that every ant heap is not necessarily inhabited by ants. When you dig in them you may find a few surprises. Therefore who knows what future science may not turn up for us.'

– – – – – –

Despite the abundance of seafoods and the pleasure the family experienced living by the sea, the meeting with the fuzimo decided them to move inland.

Next day Joha led the way through the palm trees, veered away from the sandy beach leaving the sea at his back, and was glad to hear his inner voice agreeing with the direction taken.

By evening they had crossed a flood plain and were climbing hills on the other side. Here the first conflict with Toma occurred.

'Good water there, good food there,' he complained, pointing in the direction from which they had come where a line of vegetation below them indicated a riverbed. 'You go bad,' he concluded.

Joha remained silent. He had thought the same but his voice had sent him into the hills. They had found a spring and plenty of vegetation, nothing to complain about.

Toma however gave him no peace; Feseta too joined in her mate's niggles. She had gained in confidence, taking pleasure in making her voice heard. When Joha turned his back on them both, Toma grabbed his father angrily by the shoulder and spun him round.

Joha looked at his son long and hard. Little Toma had grown into a large muscular male towering above him, and he now wore a nasty expression on a face that had always been pleasant. So many memories flooded into Joha's brain that he felt confused: there was the day he found the toddler Toma when he thought him lost for good; the day Toma disappeared from camp; there was the stampede and earth slide; Toma's entanglement in that tree; his strange 'sleep' and awakening, and their long journey together, culminating in finding Moogi and Amu.

Toma might be right about better campsites in the plain below but it was the voice that surely knew best where to go. Joha was not giving it up now. If Toma and Feseta wanted to return to previous stops, he told them, they were free to go. Once more he turned his back to indicate he did not want to listen to any more words. The couple moved off but after a while could be seen making a shelter further down the hill.

At dawn an extraordinary sight met the rising family. At the foot of the hills an extensive lake covered the flood plain. They had experienced no rain, where had all that water come from? One thing though was clear: had they stayed where Toma had suggested, they would have been overcome by the floodwaters during the night.

When Toma and Feseta joined them, instead of expressing gratitude that Joha had not agreed to staying near the river, tension between father and son continued in constant criticism. Why did they have to move every dawn, when would they stop and make a permanent camp in a place with food and water? Toma demanded to know, and why did Joha not want to listen?

'Me big, me kill good-good flesh, me find water. Me say stay,' became Toma's standard talk. Feseta agreed with every word. Moogi looked troubled.

Joha's feet grew more painful, his hair went grey, and he lost weight so that Moogi, like Toma and Feseta, could see he was no longer the big male he imagined himself. Nevertheless the family remained together, trudging daily after Joha who showed no hesitation about the direction in which they should safari.

When they reached the top of the hills, an extensive plateau spread out before them populated by a huge troop of baboons. They were grazing like hoofed animals, or cavorting about, grooming one another amidst noisy chatter that sounded like the talk of a multitude of fuzimo. The males among them, formidably large, had long hair growing like a cape round their shoulders, which made them seem even bigger.

Joha and Toma decided they might provide succulent flesh and began their stalking tactics. To their surprise the males came galloping towards them, stopping only a few paces away. Before father and son could collect their wits the baboons stood up on their hind legs, the hairy cape spread outward about their massive shoulders like the fronds of palms, and baring their sharp fangs they barked furiously, refusing to give way.

More and more large males ran up, threatening to surround the whole family, at which point Joha shouted, 'We go!' They picked up the two children and fled pell-mell downhill through a gully, holding on to vegetation as best they could. The biggest beasts followed with furious bellows while balancing with ease on top of rocks, but kept their distance.

On reaching a valley bottom, the family could see the animals on the skyline running hither and thither on the edge of a cliff, their furious remonstrations still audible in the contrasting stillness of late afternoon. Scratched by thorn bushes and jagged rocks past which they had run, the family sat down exhausted but Joha urged them to continue their flight, as did his inner voice. They jogged on, carrying the children in turn without a halt until it was nearly dark.

Meeting the murderous fuzimo and then the huge baboons shook them out of their feeling of safety experienced along the seashore. The children no longer ran where they pleased. Amu had grown considerably and looked like her father, coarse-haired, sturdy and duskier of skin in contrast to Moogi, Feseta and Badili who all had longish black hair and lighter skins.

She had proved herself trustworthy and therefore increasingly able to look after Badili. The task of cutting branches for shelters at sunset meant that the adults were fully occupied, while Amu was left to mind her brother. Nevertheless Moogi always kept an ear open for the children's chatter, making sure they did not stray far in the hostile surroundings.

When there was silence she went to investigate. The others heard a muffled cry, desperate nevertheless, dropped what they were doing and hurried to her. At her feet was Amu head in hands, her body racked by sobs, and a little distance away a young cheetah crouched by some rocks with the lifeless looking form of Badili, one of his legs held fast in its mouth.

Not a sound came from the child. He looked dead. Joha and Toma were about to rush forward to kill the animal and retrieve the boy but Moogi, uttering a low but commanding, 'No!' stopped them. They all stood still rigid with apprehension.

In her mind a memory surfaced. She said a few words just loud enough for the others to understand. There was a moment of absolute silence, then she and Feseta began to scream, Joha and Toma roared. The cheetah, a young beast, looked round, dropped his prey and streaked away. Everybody rushed forward to Badili's side. Joha picked him up carefully, while the rest bent over him fearful that he was dead. He was however still breathing, and bleeding from the tooth marks where the animal had mauled him. Moogi taking soil into her mouth chewed it into a mud patch to cover the punctured skin on his leg.

Badili lay in his father's arms, seemingly unaware of all their attempts to jolly him into any kind of response. He did not cry, he made no sound at all and his eyes were firmly shut. Apart from the punctured leg there was no other sign of injury. Moogi sat him up and tried giving him the breast, Feseta stroked his hands, Toma talked to him about the bad-bad buhu that had now run away, and Joha looked on bewildered and sad. Badili had suddenly changed into something resembling a corpse, yet he was warm to the touch and reminded Joha of Toma before the little old fuzimo had woken him with a bad tasting drink.

Amu too was unable to speak when questioned, pitifully crying her eyes out. Toma picked her up and soothed her into telling him they had been playing with Oma when the cheetah jumped on Badili from behind, took hold of his leg and dragged him away. She thought the animal had killed him.

Eventually as nobody could do anything to improve his state, they crept into their shelters, expecting the worst by dawn. He lay cradled in Moogi's arms all night, at last finding his voice and every now and then whimpering and sobbing.

In the morning for once Joha did not listen to his urging voice. Instead he suggested they stay in camp for Badili's sake, and all that day the family sat around, anxious to hear him say some of his childish words. Amu brought Oma for him to play, Feseta tried to interest him in eating tender leaves, Moogi fed him, but apart from a few sucks he still refused all drink and food.

The voice meantime gave Joha no peace, urging him constantly to 'go'. He was torn between obeying it and staying in camp in the hope that Badili's condition might improve. It did not. He lay in his nest of soft grass mostly sleeping but on waking showed no desire to talk or play. Amu constantly brought him titbits, told him what Oma was up to, tried singing to him and skipping up and down calling to him to join her.

Joha meanwhile hunted flesh, leaving Toma to guard the camp, but some mornings later when he felt he could no longer withstand the urgency of his inner voice, he ordered, 'We go!' picked Badili up and walked away in the direction he was given.

They all took turns at carrying the boy, whose condition improved only very gradually over time. As the days passed, natural growth increased his weight so that it became more and more difficult for the adults shouldering him to walk up and down hill in the uneven terrain Joha had chosen. Toma eventually took his father aside and with great assuredness, speaking from his superior height, told him that he, Toma, was now the leading male. Joha would have to listen to his opinion that the child was only a burden to them all. Badili would never recover, the flesh had done something to him. His leg looked twisted, even when the wound healed he would never walk properly.

'He no good,' said Toma. 'You kill Badili.' Seeing his father's pained expression, Toma offered to do it himself with the cudgel.

Joha's resentment of Toma's behaviour spilled over. 'No!' he roared, so that the others turned to see what was happening. 'Me tell you,' and in his anger words spilled out of him in short phrases as never before. He related how Toma had left them a long time ago, something he obviously never remembered, how there had been a stampede of animals in which he lost Moogi and Amu, how the earth shook, how trees had fallen over and slid downhill, how he found Toma caught up in one and asleep, and he demonstrated hanging on to branches as they were carried at great speed to even ground.

'You sleep-sleep,' Joha told Toma accusingly. 'Me carry you, dawn, dawn, dawn. Me no kill you. Me carry, carry, carry!' and he almost spat the words at his hulk of a son in his fury.

'Me wake?' Toma asked suddenly subdued, as his father told them all how he had never opened his eyes until the old fuzimo poured a drink down his throat.

The others gathered round, listening to the strange tale. Moogi and Feseta who had never heard the story looked at each other with astonishment.

'You carry Toma?' Feseta asked incredulously. Moogi too observed how their size had changed, Joha being the one so thin where Toma was now broad and tall.

'You good-good!' she exclaimed again and again in admiration of her male, the others echoing her words. 'Joha good-good.'

Toma listening intently, asked questions and sat looking at none of them, all his feelings of superiority gradually vanishing as his father found words to describe a past the others had not heard about and he had only vaguely understood from what Joha had told him after their stay with the old fuzimo and child.

At the end of his tale Joha turned to Badili who had been listening to the angry words without understanding what was going on, took his hand and looking at him intently said, 'You Badili for me!' From then on he carried the boy as often and long as his strength permitted, ignoring Toma when he came up begging to help.

Joha never forgot Toma's original suggestion that Badili could be killed with a blow of the cudgel.

Although Badili eventually recovered from the paralysing fright, the leg as predicted never grew straight. His previous running gait turned into a hobble, one leg shorter than the other.

After marching many dawns, Joha leading in the direction of his voice's commands, they left the hills behind and found palms, sand and ocean once more. Moogi the water lover ran to embrace the waves, to frolic and laugh, and splash her children, while the others looked for the shell-foods they had already tasted during their previous encounter with the sea. Badili tottered into the water, gave a hoot of delight and immediately began swimming about, his shorter leg no longer a hindrance to movement. Amu, Toma and Feseta too, were able swimmers by now and only Joha went no further than immersing his very sore feet.

The young couple forgot all talk of returning to previous favourite camps. Life had been made easy by finding crops of seaweed and oysters as they journeyed along beaches interrupted only by freshwater streams easily fordable. Rock pools allowed foraging for fish and crabs.

One day dusk set in just as they reached the top of a hump of dunes. The last of the sun's rays glistened on sandbanks and lit up small islands offshore. A faint opposite shoreline quickly merged with the sky in the fading light. They made camp, brought out seafoods from their bags and told each other, 'This good-good!'

At dawn Joha found them a spring to replenish the gourds, and just as the others were ready to go and looked at him to lead them out of camp, he sat down with his back against a large stone.

'Me no go,' he said.

The statement took the others by complete surprise. Down went hunting sticks, bolas, cudgels, gourds and food bags. Everybody came up to see what was wrong. Moogi especially, noticed how emaciated he was.

Amu immediately went to him, leaned down to grasp his hand in both hers and asked solicitously, 'You no go?'

'No!'

It only took her a moment of decision. Pushing Oma out of a food pouch where she had just put it in preparation for the continued journey, she placed the tortoise beside her father's sore feet.

'We go,' she announced to the others, imitating the way Joha had always led them, and pointed her small hand towards the islands and the further shore now clearly visible under the morning sun.

Joha gave her a searching look. 'You hear?'

'Me hear,' she assured him, and ran to the water's edge, waded into the sea and began swimming towards the first sandbank. Badili not to be outdone ran as best he could after her and plunged in too. Moogi glancing from Joha to her children, decided she must follow and find out what Amu meant.

Toma looked at his father, worn out, feet sore, eyes shut, and leaning on the big stone.

'You stay?' he asked uncertainly, but Joha did not answer. He seemed to be taking a rest.

'We go, come back for you,' Toma said kindly and beckoning to Feseta, they walked out of Africa into the shallow sea and swam away to join the others.

Part of *UKUnpublished.co.uk*   .CO.UK

UKBookland gives you the opportunity to purchase all of the books
published by UKUnpublished.

Do you want to find out a bit more about your favourite UKUnpublished
Author?

Find other books they have written?

**PLUS – UKBookland offers all the books at Excellent Discounts to the
Recommended Retail Price!**

You can find UKBookland at www.ukbookland.co.uk

Find out more about **Edith Cory-King** and her books.

Are you an Author?

Do you want to see your book in print?

Please look at the UKUnpublished website:
www.ukunpublished.co.uk

Let the World Share Your Imagination

Lightning Source UK Ltd.
Milton Keynes UK
19 March 2010

151579UK00001B/7/P